The Elements of Time

Time travel stories by Duncan Lunan

Illustrated by Sydney Jordan

First published as *With Time Comes Concord and Other Stories*,
edited by Gary Gibson, Brain in a Jar Books, 2012; revised,
illustrated and expanded, Shoreline of Infinity, 2016.

The Elements of Time
Duncan Lunan

Published by Shoreline of Infinity Publications

(The New Curiosity Shop)

www.shorelineofinfinity.com

ISBN 978-0-9934413-5-6

Designed and Typeset by The New Curiosity Shop

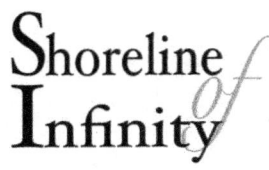

To those who helped with these
stories and are no longer with us:
Ken Bowyer, John Braithwaite, Chris Boyce,
Alasdair Lunan, Bill Roberts and Archie Roy.

Contents

The Day and the Hour. First published in *Celtic Warrior*, 1976; revised version in *There Will Be War, Vol.5: Warrior!*, ed. Jerry Pournelle & John F. Carr, Tor Books, 1986; trans. Fenix Publications, Poland.

In the Arctic, Out of Time. First published as cover story, *Isaac Asimov's Science Fiction Magazine*, July 1989; trans. Fenix Publications, Poland.

With Time Comes Concord. First published in *Analog Science Fiction/Science Fact*, September 1993.

Riding the Fire. Provisionally accepted by *Amazing Stories*, 1994, but unused because the magazine ceased publication. First published in *With Time Comes Concord and Other Stories*, ed. Gary Gibson, Brain in a Jar, 2012.

Verdict of History. First published in *Dream Magazine*, July 1987; reprinted in *West Coast Magazine*, No.8 (June 1991); trans. Fenix Publications, Poland.

Faces Bearing the Stamp of Time. First published in *With Time Comes Concord and Other Stories*, Brain in a Jar, 2012.

Galileo at the High Frontier. First published in *To Arrive at Where We Started*, ed. Laura Smith, Centre for Contemporary Arts, Glasgow, August 2012.

The Day and the Hour

There was no snow to delay the unit's journey north from Salisbury. Though the stratosphere was still hazed with ice crystals, long-lived reminders of the jet aircraft now so scarce, and though veils of dust persisted still higher from the aftermath of World War Three, as the second century after the war wore on the 'years without a summer' were becoming less common. The transporter and escorts travelled all night, and came into Derby under a grey morning sky.

Johnson was taken to the General almost at once, and that in itself showed the seriousness of the situation. He had tried for years to gain the attention of the upper ranks in the British People's Army to point out the implications of his discoveries and gain recognition and priority for the research, but always he had been blocked far down the chain of command. Major Gregory, as he then was, had been one of the first disbelievers to bar Johnson's way. Since then Gregory had changed his name to Gregori, and risen through the higher echelons into supreme command of the remaining British forces. Now some twist in the national emergency had reminded Gregori of Regressive Ballistics, and Johnson was being rushed to this meeting as if he alone could save the State.

"Captain Johnson, sir." The aide saluted and withdrew.

"You've made good time from Wiltshire, Captain. Come in, take a chair." Promotion had been kind to Gregori: he had gained weight and lost hair since Johnson met him last, but it looked well on him. Yet in his years in the backwater of research, Johnson's constant struggle for funding had made him hypersensitive to the moods of his superior officers, and behind Gregori's authority he sensed a profound—disquiet?—discontent? "It looks as if we'll be in action in a few hours, so you'd better rest while you can."

"The Highlanders are still moving south, sir?"

"They are, Johnson. They stopped yesterday, but they were past Sheffield at first light today. Their mobility, I grieve to say, exceeds ours."

Johnson was shocked. Of course there had been rumours, dismissed as attempts of reactionaries to undermine the confidence of loyal soldiers, and he himself had never credited them..." A ragged peasant army, outmanoeuvring and outflanking the troops of the Soviet? Sir, I can't believe that!"

"Your pride in the armies of the Soviet does you credit," said Gregori. Was that—could it be—a hint of sarcasm? "Unfortunately, Captain, once they got through the Scottish lowlands there were relatively few of our glorious troops to oppose them. Most of our units in the north of England have been despatched to the continent, just as they were when the Young Pretender marched into England in 1745. As well as the trouble in Spain, which may do for the USSR what it did once for Napoleon, we are holding down both Hungary and Czechoslovakia yet again. As for Poland—you were going to say, Captain?"

Johnson had been through enough political education classes to think he knew a test when he saw one. "Surely, sir, on Marx's progressive view of history, the fluctuations of the dying monarchies have no relationship—"

Gregori cut him off with an impatient wave of his hand. "Much as we admire the progressive view of history, Captain, as practical military men we must consider the possibility that history may *appear* to repeat itself. It's apparent that there are two clear historical precedents for the situation facing us: the Jacobite rebellion, as I said, and before that—before that, Captain, are you a drinking man?"

To Johnson's amazement, Gregori yanked open a filing cabinet drawer to reveal a bottle of vodka and two elegant glasses, which he transferred to the desk top with slightly too steady a hand. Had he been brought all this way overnight just to be put through elementary tests of character and political soundness by the commanding General of the People's Army? "Never, sir, while on duty," he answered woodenly.

"As you please," said Gregori, pouring himself a large measure. He half-turned to indicate the map of the British Isles on the wall behind him. "Perhaps you have been too engrossed in your research to mark a disturbing trend in recent years. Increasingly the troops of other Soviet states have been withdrawn from Britain to suppress counter-revolutionary developments in Europe and Scandinavia. Now the British People's Army is taking over those security operations in Europe, while other Soviet troops are withdrawn to protect the Russian homeland from the barbarians in the ruins of Germany. Their attacks across the wastelands are becoming ever more serious. In short, Captain, our leaders in Moscow are calling the legions home." He waved at the bottle. "Still sure you won't join me?"

"No, thank you, sir." One of us has to keep a grip on reality, thought Johnson. He would have put the whole line of conversation down to the vodka, were Gregori's hands and voice not so steady. Nevertheless, as Gregori topped his own glass, the explanation was turning into a lecture.

"As I said before, Captain, we military men must take a pragmatic view of history. Rome had troubles remarkably similar to ours. They never mastered Scotland, 'Never conquered and not likely to be.' Though we've held Britain for a hundred and fifty years we've never been supreme beyond the Firths of Forth and Clyde. If we ever hoped to integrate that area with the USSR, the two bombs in the west of Scotland were a strategic mistake: if we had to do that we shouldn't have left Glasgow standing in between. The first two battalions of the brigade we sent in to occupy the Glasgow area disappeared in a manner unknown to military history since the Ninth Legion went north from the Wall."

He struck the map for emphasis. "When Castro looked at the map of Britain he cried, "Ah, Scotland! The mountains!" Unfortunately the mountains remained in the hands of counter-revolutionaries. When the first punitive expedition went north from Edinburgh, after the eight months it took to clear the commandos out of the tunnels under the Castle there, it got precisely halfway across the Forth Road Bridge and then went crashing to the sea-bed. It was rumoured at the time that they hadn't paid the toll. And so things continued in the Highlands to the present day, with the clan structure reforming as an underground movement, the old regiments regenerating as guerrilla groups and arming themselves at our expense. Often they do better than we do with our own weapons; your 'dirty wee Pict' is proving himself deadly at close quarters with a laser bayonet. You have Glaswegians treating it as a big brother to the photon flick-knife. It's my opinion, comparing this rising with Bonnie Prince Charlie's, that if the Scots get past Derby this time they'll never be stopped."

This was too much for Johnson. "Oh. come now, sir. Reinforcements..."

"There will be no reinforcements," Gregori said grimly, staring into his glass. "Oh, some heavy machines are coming north from outside London. But there are no aircraft to lift them to us and they won't reach us in time to do any good. The Scots will go round them, as they did the armour in the north of England, if they pass us here. All the troops we can spare from the south-east are already here, little more than a division, all told."

So few! Johnson could scarcely believe it. But if it was true it would have been kept quiet…and it would explain why the budget for research was vanishingly small. "But sir? What about the troops from the West Country—there are two regiments almost on our doorstep…"

"The West Country is in arms," said Gregori. "Drake's Drum, they say, is sounding again. Drake—the bourgeois adventurer, a pioneer of the capitalist era! They've a good marching song down there, I hear—whoever Trelawny was, we shouldn't have shot him."

"What about the Welsh regiments—"

"Changing sides, I believe. Richard the Second had some trouble of the same kind, and as for Wales itself, they have the precedent of Owen Glendower—who outdid Ché himself, since Glendower was never caught. When the English claimed no invasions since 1066, we were already thinking of Britain as a unit. At the moment it seems that all the historical rebellions are recurring at once."

Johnson was aghast. For all his skill in interpreting and exploiting the attitudes of senior officers—a survival skill, for the continuation of his research—he had remained a scientist, untouched by politics within the army or outside. What he saw in Gregori was an Englishman who had spent his life in the effort to become a Russian and now suspected—incredibly, to Johnson— that he might have chosen the wrong side. Why had Gregori brought him here? Had the General perceived some way in which he, a humble captain in research, could save the revolution in England?

"Now you know how bad it is," said Gregori. "The battle here in a few hours may stem the tide. If we lose, I think this is the beginning of the end for the revolution, for the unity of Europe and for the USSR as we know it. In our desire to extend that revolution over all the globe, we've overstretched our resources— technically, militarily and economically. It would have been easier to colonise the Moon than to reclaim North America after the Last War, as we optimistically named it. But we—Russia—panicked when we had a temporary advantage, and Russia's guilt, Russia's attempted reparation, has ruined us all. We're standing here today against the new Dark Ages, Captain, and we're going to lose because we're so few. Your discovery may serve to swing the balance, as a last desperate chance. Can you do it?"

"I don't know, sir," Johnson stammered, caught unprepared in the middle of his analysis of Gregori. "It's only a prototype ...successful in a few controlled tests, untried in battle conditions

....the paradoxes—"

"Courage, Captain! For the revolution, for the Soviet, for the future of the world, today you stand in the breach!" Outright sarcasm—not just the vodka. "Your field works. You can project a shell backwards in time?"

"Regressive Ballistics, sir. We can fire a shell through the field generated in front of the tank, and it will move backwards through time as its trajectory continues. At the maximum range of the gun we have, the shell is displaced only an hour into the past."

"That hour may be enough, Captain," said Gregori. "We shall fight ferociously, of course, but if we can last an hour against the Scottish horde I shall be surprised. Over the battle, however, Remotely Piloted Vehicles will record everything for transmission to my command post, and as we and our computers analyse the battle we shall transmit the edited highlights to you. An hour after battle is joined, you will know which elements in the enemy advance were to prove crucial; and on the empty battlefield, you will fire the shells that are to change history."

"But sir, the firepower of our prototype rig—"

"If you recall, Captain, I asked for your shell specifications to be radioed ahead. Just an hour ago, an aircraft arrived from Moscow with a consignment of the latest antimatter shells, specially made for your puny gun." Gregori hefted the vodka bottle. "This came with them, unrequested: intended as a farewell gift, I suspect... but we shall see. It's just as well the explosions will be an hour in the past if your range is what you've reported! Was 120mm the heaviest piece you could requisition?"

"We couldn't get any guns at all for research, sir. We...we dug this one out of the ground."

"Out of the ground! What, a wreck from the Battle of Stonehenge?"

"Yes, sir. The radioactivity's almost gone now, of course, but it took quite a while to make it serviceable."

"It must have done," said Gregori, with respect. "My confidence in you is restored, Captain. I was beginning to put you down as a mere researcher, lacking in initiative. Perhaps if anyone can turn the tide of history... But the field itself, the projector. You mentioned a tank. Not something that will take hours to set up, I trust—a tank of oil? Not liquid helium!"

"Not a tank *of* anything, sir," Johnson explained, still more embarrassed. "A tank in the historical sense: a manned armoured vehicle, with rotating turret for low-powered cannon."

Gregori was fascinated. "Propulsion?"

"Caterpillar tracks only, sir. Diesel engine."

"And I was lecturing you on military history. It's a real museum piece, the forerunner of today's military armour?"

"Yes, indeed, sir. It's an FV 4030 Challenger, once the most advanced fighting machine of its day. Its type were entering service with the British Army in 1985 as successors to the Chieftain series—incorporating the same armament and integrated Fire Control System, but with Chobham armour and a mere powerful engine." Johnson could have warmed to his subject, but that was a prerogative for superior officers.

"This is excellent," said Gregori. "So you don't have just a temperamental prototype, you have a mobile combat unit, however antiquated. Its antiquity may even be an advantage—it may let you pass the advancing Scots without attracting attention. Lenin knows what they'll take it to be, but the idea that it's a threat will escape them—especially since it'll be crawling on to the field of their victory!"

"You realise, sir, that the tank doesn't have anything like its former turn of speed. Once it could exceed fifty-six kilometres per hour, but not now."

"So much the better, to avoid attracting attention. We'll have you behind the lines, under deep camouflage. The Highlanders will be able to storm right ever the top of you by the time our experts have finished. But afterwards, when battle ends, we'll give you a sonic pulse from divisional HQ to move forward. If I can

I'll join you myself to direct your fire—if not, Captain, you must assess the battle's course for yourself and destroy the key Scottish units."

When shall we next meet again? wondered Gregori, when Johnson had gone. *When the battle's lost and won?* The idea was fantastic; yet the chance was there to save the State and his own career, very probably his neck. The best of it was that he could make good his escape, in that Russian aircraft, when defeat became certain—and if Johnson reversed the outcome, the General would thereby be restored to his post, ready to claim the rewards of the otherwise unattainable victory. If Johnson achieved nothing, General Gregori would have escaped shellfire, firing squad or prison camp and be on his way to a new life. But where was he to go, he wondered, standing before the map with vodka glass in hand like an English Roman in his villa, nursing the last cup of wine from Italy when the galleys had gone. Where was his refuge to be?

Ireland?

Now's the day and now's the hour:
See the front of battle lour:
See approach proud Edward's power,
Chains and slaverie.

Robert Bums, "Scots Wha Hae".

1500 hours (A): Sergeant Macdonald of the Cameron Highlanders Artillery, Blue Section, finished the deployment of his guns. They were Russian mobile cannon, captured in the Lowlands after the second battle of Prestonpans: relatively light, they could be shifted swiftly on air cushions to come to bear on new targets. Against the armoured division barring the way to Derby their firepower would be well-nigh ineffective, but ostensibly their function was to provide covering fire for the Scots commandos, to help to pin down whatever troops the English had mustered, while the teams moved in and the shaped charges were placed. Unless the massive fighting machines of the People's Army could be knocked out, with their superior range and firepower they could hold England from the Pennines to the Wash. The Scottish army had had to split up for the night dash that brought them close enough to do battle, or those juggernauts might have blown them apart at Sheffield, forty miles away.

Macdonald checked again, though their position was the best possible. On the right-hand tip of the Highland crescent, well forward but aside from the heaviest fighting, they could provide crossfire and also spot targets for the more substantial Highland artillery. That was their true function, though other such units spaced out along the line and providing covering fire would conceal the fact. Blue Section's true task was to spotlight, at the right time and not before, what the English were holding in reserve and when the outgunned Scots *must* take it out.

He lowered himself briefly from the slit to the controls of the command unit, to glance back at the youth at the impact predictor panel. "All set, Alastair?"

The lad swallowed hard. "It's shaping up nicely, Sergeant." The flickering colours of the computer display chased across his pale face.

"Fair enough." Macdonald picked up the hand mike. "Dheargh Mhatan to Claymore—activated and ready."

"Stand by, Dheargh Mhatan."

In the First, Second and Third World Wars, the Scots had been known to their enemies as "Demons in Skirts", "Ladies from Hell", and "Poison Dwarves." One of their demonic tricks had been to use Gaelic on the radio when they might be overheard. This army's mix of English-speaking Lowlanders meant that Gaelic was used only for code-words, but that would be enough to keep the English guessing. "Claymore" was Lochiel himself, commanding the Scottish push south as once his ancestor had advised Prince Charles Edward in the same desperate game. It was no accident that he had taken for his call-sign a word which had been *claidheamh mòr*, a great sword, and had been applied to more than three types of deadly weapon.

"Claymore to all units—Caber Feidh is sounded. Dheargh Mhatan, do you hear?"

Macdonald smiled. *Caber Feidh* was the old regimental march of the Seaforths: when it was sounded on the pipes in a situation like this, they would be advancing into battle. An Englishman listening would probably think it was a place which had been checked out. There was a check-out in progress, but of a very different kind: after another glance towards Alastair, Macdonald again raised the mike.

"We hear, Claymore—Caber Feidh is quite clear."

If anyone out there knows pipe music, Macdonald told himself, let them think we're having a concert. They'll dance to our tune soon enough.

"Claymore to Hielan' Laddie: Bundle and Go. March, March, Ettrick and Teviotdale!"

That was the Black Watch committed; and now, the King's Own Scottish Borderers. The Black Watch should have been in Macdonald's direct field of view, and as he stood up to the slit his movement-sensitive scope picked out the infantry moving through the trees on their jet-packs, their suits dialled to winter camouflage tartan.

"Alert for Hielan' Laddie," said Alastair. Guided by the screen display, Alastair was now locked on to the advancing troops with strange powers of his own, tracking them and projecting their track forward into the future. His trance lasted only seconds. "Two machine-gun posts, automated, concealed half-a-mile ahead of them. They'll open fire in sixty-five seconds. I'm laying-in the target now."

"We can take care of those ourselves, it doesn't need heavy bombardment. We'll do it now and clear your view for the next hazard." As Macdonald spoke, the guns of Blue Section were swinging towards the target Alastair had pinpointed. "Two rounds each, fire at will."

Sergeant Macdonald was a reliable NCO picked by Lochiel for his lack of imagination. He accepted Alastair's gift of the Second Sight as he might accept that another man could paint, or play the fiddle. Told by the young Adept of the threats the near future held, he would act to counter them without questioning the information; without raising an atmosphere of doubt that might blur Alastair's predictions. The boy was Lochiel's secret weapon, trained in the Western Isles by agents brought by submarine from the unknown base of the American government in exile. Personally, Sergeant Macdonald had no time for the new jargon of *Adepts* and *Psionics*; privately he doubted the value of the training, which had sharpened Alastair's erratic gift into a practical tool of warfare but had unnerved the lad, particularly in combat. To Macdonald, who had known him since childhood, it was a good soldier spoiled. But he wouldn't question what Alastair told him, and he would act on it as a trained soldier. And that made him an ideal anchor for the Adept.

1525 hrs. (A): It had fallen to MacDonald's unit to open the battle, despite their orders to keep a low profile. But with troops already committed across so much of the battlefield, it could have happened anywhere, and fire-fights swiftly broke out all along the front. The enemy's fighting vehicles, huge Russian machines which in another age would have been big enough to carry moon-rockets to their pads, ground slowly forward from cover to meet the Highlanders with firepower nothing on Earth could resist. They had been developed after the Last War, when the armoured divisions of both sides were annihilated in the tactical holocaust of Germany. Only a direct nuclear hit would destroy them. But the Black Watch had been working their way up, making use of smokescreens and barrages laid down for other parts of the battle. Given their timing by Alastair, they rushed a nearby hill and plastered the war machines with old-fashioned anti-tank missiles, while the commandos made their suicide runs to plant the shaped nuclear charges. The troops took heavy losses, despite the covering fire from Blue Section and its counterparts; but the land dreadnoughts were stopped or at even disabled, with their fields of fire consequently restricted, and one by one the commandos took them out.

1545 hrs. (A): Such was the firepower of modem armies, an engagement that might once have lasted hours was already over. Casualties had been fearsome: it might be said that the Scots had won only in the sense that they still had some men and guns left when the People's Army was annihilated. But there would be reinforcements within hours, now that the North was up and taking arms; and prompted perhaps by the Scottish success, Welsh forces were leaving the mountains against Wolverhampton, Worcester and Gloucester. The heavy Soviet armour coming from London was in trouble with guerrillas at St. Albans. All Lochiel's army had to do was occupy Derby and hold it.

"Dheargh Mhatan from Claymore, Dheargh Mhatan from Claymore, clear us a path into the town. We'll be mopping up behind you."

"Dheargh Mhatan, aye. Leader to all Blue Section units, prepare to move off!"

They breasted the rise ahead, swung round the burning wreck of a war machine in the field beyond, and roared down to the main road. Taking up line astern, they put down their heavy drive wheels, shutting off ground effect. They met no trouble on the way in; surviving units of the People's Army, hands raised, were left to surrender to the main force. The news of their coming spread like wildfire from the outskirts of Derby: by the time they neared the town centre, cheering crowds were lining the route. Macdonald saw in the rear scanner that Fraser in No.2, defying snipers, was up in the hatch with the pipes. The external microphone picked up *The March of the Cameron Men.*

As said before, Macdonald was not imaginative, but the historical significance of the moment wasn't lost on him. Turning over the controls to his co-driver, he too stood up at the observation slit and threw open the top hatch. Out among the cheering, with the Cameron pennants fluttering before him on the whip aerials, tradition really got to him. As they entered the centre of Derby he took off his tin hat and flourished it in triumph, shouting "The

Prince is coming! The Prince is coming!"

1550 hrs. (A): Though the Highland army was passing on both sides, regrouping as they went for the march into Derby, a dreadful quiet occupied the battlefield. Johnson had never seen active service, not even skirmishes with the small forces China could still miraculously generate after all this time. There hadn't been as devastating an engagement as this within living memory.

Though the sonic pulse hadn't come, and neither had Gregori, he couldn't wait in hiding any longer. His shells could go back only an hour in time, and to hit the Black Watch (unfamiliar with the tartans, he had classified them "X group") before they got too close to the front line of the People's Army, his little team would have to move. He pushed a button, and the heavier parts of their camouflage parted explosively above them. Among the ruins of the armoured division, that little bang would never be noticed. Their treads bit into the earth ramp, and the tank heaved up towards the winter sky.

The rearguard of the Highland army, passing at speed to left and right, took no notice of the Challenger as it rumbled down a clear alley between the flaming war machines to the fields beyond. Why should they? The least of the weapon-carriers, lesser, captured units though they were, dwarfed it. If it weren't for the gun it might almost pass as some kind of a lifeboat, or tender for the stricken giants nearby: and the gun was no threat, pointing to where the Highlanders had come from, not where they were now. If any of the infantry swooping along on their jet-packs swerved to check it out, they were reassured by the saltires which Gregori had suggested be flown from the turret aerials.

Though it had been convenient to have the gun and projector mobile for the trials on Salisbury Plain, Johnson had never ridden in the tank himself. The noise and vibration appalled him. How people had managed to fight these machines at speed, with what precision the crude instruments of 1985 afforded, he couldn't see. He wasn't even able to follow the RPV record when he tried to re-check his interpretation of the battle.

1610 hrs. (A): They were in position. The time projector was on, its antennae extended to engage the shell at the focus of the field, as it left the barrel. Johnson was at the contra-rotating cupola periscope, his left eye to the roll-ball, split field monocular sighting in real-time. The overhead film of the battle, now synchronised to exactly one hour in the past, was presented to his right eye by a modem holographic head-up display, from whose reference grid he could read off the range. He adjusted the antique tank helmet, checked position of throat mike and ear muffs, and cleared his throat.

"Target range 800 metres. Antimatter, one round. Come to bear."

The old gun swung in traverse and elevation, locking (as accurately as its guidance system would allow) on to the Black Watch advance an hour before. With these blockbuster shells, any lack of precision there would be quite academic. The field had better work, Johnson told himself, or we'll blow ourselves right off the hillside at this range.

"Fixed," said the gunner. Two tracers flashed from the ranging machine gun, off into the empty fields. The electronics of the tank's laser ranging system had been knocked out by electromagnetic pulse 150 years before, and there was no chance of replacements from Barr & Stroud in Glasgow—but in this case, the older method was what was needed. There was no target for laser and infrared sensors out there, only the images on the synchronised record, about to become ghosts in every sense.

"On target," said Johnson. The old command sequence gave him a feeling of continuity with the: traditions of the British Army. Marlborough, Wellington—no, perhaps not. At 1611 (A) precisely, he ordered, "Fire!"

1512 hrs. (B) (the projector wasn't quite at maximum range); Sgt. Macdonald had just received confirmation from Observer Ewan Cameron that the machine-gun posts were destroyed, when there was a colossal flash of light about a mile to the east. By sheer luck he happened not to be looking directly into it, but half his vision was filled with after images. Though the command unit's shock absorbers coped, the sway relative to the ground outside was plainly visible. Beyond the Black Watch advance, which must have been wiped out, the bare winter trees had come down: those nearest to ground zero were still standing, but furiously ablaze.

"Dheargh Mhatan to Claymore, Dheargh Mhatan to Claymore—nuclear strike on Hielan' Laddie. Hielan' Laddie is taken out. They must have read Lochiel's mind!" he added after switching off. Macdonald's soft Highland accent, subdued by years of shouted orders, was brought out by his anger,

"That can only have been antimatter," his co-driver said from the instrument panel. "They must have stunned their own front line, using it at that range."

"Aye," Macdonald dropped from the slit, twisting out of the seat to face Alastair. In the cramped interior of the Command Unit, that put him only a foot from the Adept.

"I didn't see it, Sergeant!" Alastair was distraught at his failure. "I didn't even see the shell coming!"

"Never mind, lad," said Macdonald, boiling. "Where did it come from?"

Alastair looked desperate, but said his piece. "That hillside there, Sergeant—right in front of us. I can feel it. But the detectors show nothing there..."

"Our own eyes show nothing there!" Macdonald twisted himself viciously left, then right, back up to the slit. "There's *bugger-all* there," he hissed. "Nevertheless, lay it in..."

Blue Section's guns roared together. At that range it was almost a flat trajectory. The hillside facing them split open, again and again.

1613 hrs. (B): Johnson had been watching the synchronised record eagerly, expecting to see the flash of the shell interrupt the sequence he had followed earlier. But no, the advance went on as before. For a terrible moment he feared failure; but looking up, he found the battlefield had changed, though the record paradoxically remained the same. The ruined formation of war machines had overtaken him, though they had been destroyed in the end; their burning wreckage lay along the top of the slope, one or two further forward on his right where the ground levelled out. And the Highland rearguard had been pushed back; though still victorious, the units now passing him were fewer and slower. Casualties were heavier, damage more severe. He had changed the course of the battle, though his records of it were unaltered. After a moment he realised that his recording of the last hour must remain unchanged, or memory too would have gone. This was the first of the paradoxes he had feared when transferring his half-completed research project to the front.

He would have to act fast if the new course of recent events, of which he had no record, was not to diverge too far from the previous track still running on the synchronised display. He had the Challenger's gun fixed on the next target when suddenly his situation changed. Though he felt nothing, there was a discontinuity in his perceptions: the tank was nose-down and there was less light coming in. The periscope showed that now they were lying at the bottom of a deep crater, the gun almost in the earth. For another dreadful moment he thought that the time-projector antennae had been smashed, but they were just clear of the fresh-turned soil.

So the Highlanders had 'spotted' him! It would do them no good. An hour in their future, nothing they did could touch him. A sense of real power possessed Johnson. He alone would save the Soviet State of Britain. But he must move fast, or his next shell might light on the advancing English front line in the new past he had created. The driver restarted the engine, engaged the caterpillar tracks, and began to reverse up the steep slope of the crater.

1515 hrs. (B): The smoke had cleared on the hillside blasted by Blue Section's bombardment. Macdonald was scanning the pattern of craters. "We've dug nothing up there," he said, but without scepticism.

"Sergeant..." Alastair began uncertainly. He was sitting back from the computer display, eyes glazed again.

Macdonald continued scanning. "What, lad?"

"Sergeant, I can see that shell now."

"Yes?"

"I don't...you'll not..."

Macdonald dropped and swung out of the chair again. Whatever the Sight revealed, by God he had to know it. Very gently, he took hold of the tranced Adept by the lapels of his battledress. The Highland accent still more noticeable, he said slowly and forcefully, with even a hint of menace, "Alastair, tell me what you see!"

"Just the shell, Sergeant. As if it were going backwards from its target to the hillside. I can still only see the nearest part of its trajectory. It's up there, right now, with us in time!"

Sergeant Macdonald was not imaginative. He accepted that Alastair could see what he himself could not, and was not plagued by the kind of doubt which could argue or interfere with that source of information. His technical education told him that matter going backwards in time could look like antimatter coming forwards, and vice versa—the words 'Feynman diagram' were at the back of his mind somewhere, but if Alastair described it, Macdonald took his word for it.

"Oh, the bastards," he said quietly. That the English could send shells backwards through time came as no great surprise to him. The English were capable of anything. "You can see into the future, lad," he went on as quietly as before. "You can see that launcher. When will it be there?"

"I can't see it," said Alastair, turning his head from side to side in mental anguish. "It's as if the future that shell came from has been wiped away...."

"The shell itself gives you a link," Macdonald said, soothing, directing the Adept's attention. "Just tell me, lad, when will it 'return' to that hillside?"

Alastair said nothing. He began to tremble in his seat.

"Switch everything off," snapped Macdonald. "No talking, no distractions." The shifting patterns of the computer display died. Alastair's powers alone linked him to the battle.

"An hour from now, nearly," he gasped, and snapped out of the trance, weeping from the strain.

"That's all we need to know..." The satisfaction in Macdonald's voice was filled with menace now, as he swung back to the control position. "Switches on!...Lachlan, we want a barrage fused to explode in one hour. Make it fast."

"But Sergeant, our delay fuses only run in seconds," the armourer protested over the intercom from No. 3 gun.

"So fix me some for thirty-six hundred seconds," said Macdonald, some of the menace transferred from the enemy. "One round at a time if need be. Let me know when you're *ready*, Lachie ..." He switched off, turning to the recovering Adept. "Don't you worry, laddie. To make an explosion an hour before you in time may be the work of the devil, but to plant one an hour in time behind you is an old, established art."

1555 hrs. (B): Lachlan's old, established art seemed to have won the contest. Correcting the fuse settings to get an approximately simultaneous detonation, No. 3 gun had sown the mangled hillside with a broad pattern of shells. No more disabling fire had come back from the future, and the battle had raged on. Alastair's warnings didn't completely forestall the war machines' contribution, but one by one they had been immobilised by suicide squads and hammered out of the action. The Highland army had survived, though drastically weakened; and Lochiel ordered Macdonald to enter Derby at once, to consolidate the victory.

"Prepare to move off," said Macdonald. "No. 4: in about twenty-three minutes our charges should go off in that hillside. Get you into the cover of those trees and watch. If by any chance we failed to catch the devilish contrivance that will appear there, don't you make any mistake with it." Blue Section started up on their air cushions, moving down into the valley. Only No. 4 gun separated from them, moving along the top of the rise into the trees.

1600 hrs. (B): Ewan Cameron saw the ancient Challenger trundling up the field to the hillside opposite. He could scarcely believe his eyes, and one by one his crew snatched quick looks to confirm it. Only the knowledge that the shambling tank with its false saltires could have turned the battle gave strain to their laughter. The tank nosed over the brow of the hill, than came to rest apparently poised over one of the craters. It seemed as if there had to be solid ground below it, yet to Ewan it seemed at the same time that the tank hung over empty air. After some delay, two silvery antennae were extended parallel to the old-fashioned gun barrel, and twisted to focus on the space just before the muzzle. The gun swung, then slowly began to track the movements of the Black Watch an hour before. Though he watched carefully, Ewan was certain afterwards that he didn't see the first shell fired—a paradox that would have interested Johnson. At 1614, however, for no apparent reason, the Challenger's invisible support was no longer there and the tank itself was suddenly almost out of sight, nose down in the crater. When it came out No. 4 gun was laid in, in case there should be any mistake. But at 1622, just when the tank gun was locked on its next target and Ewan himself was about to fire, the hillside erupted once more. Two charges went off directly below the Challenger: it was blown high into the air, its treads disintegrating as it turned over. The gun flailed and the turret flew off. The tank fell, burning, and after the impact came three brilliant explosions, each bigger than the last.

No. 4 gun was overturned by the blast and hammered into the hillside; and though only the first flash had pierced Ewan's polaroid goggles, it would be days before his eyes were unbandaged. Still it was with great cheer that the crew extricated themselves from the wreckage and set off on foot, following the Highland army's advance into Derby.

Notes

The first three stories in this collection, featuring time travel by land, sea and air, all have long and complicated histories, stretching back to the 1960s. They are particular favourites of mine, however, so I feel that the struggle to see them into print has been worthwhile.

The main idea of 'The Day and the Hour' arose in a Logic tutorial essay for the Philosophy Department of the University of Glasgow. The text was from the section on 'Memory' in "The Problem of Knowledge" by A.J. Ayer (Penguin, 1956):

"But what is it that prevents one from recapturing a past experience? With the progress of science, why should not a time machine be constructible which would enable us to travel in time, as we already succeed in travelling in space? Why should one not literally relive the scenes of one's childhood, or, for that matter, enjoy in advance the experiences of one's old age? It may not be technically feasible, but surely the possibility can at least be envisaged. Has it not, indeed, already been envisaged by writers of science fiction? The answer to this is that there is no difficulty at all in supposing that one can have experiences which are exactly like the experiences of one's childhood: one can conceive of their being obtained through hypnotism, or the use of drugs; there is no need to have recourse to anything so dubious as a time machine. But they still would not be the same experiences; and the reason why they would not be the same is just that they would occur at a different date. Even if it were possible to have one's life over and over again, in the sense that whenever one reached a certain age one would proceed to undergo a series of experiences which were qualitatively the same in every detail as those that one had undergone since birth, this still would not constitute a literal recapture of the past. One term of the cycle would be necessarily different from one another. There is, therefore, no possibility of travelling in time. To travel in space is to be at different places at different times; but the idea of being at different times at different times is simply nonsensical. One can imagine being projected back to the eighteenth century, in the sense that from a given moment onwards one would have only such experiences as would be appropriate to that period of history; but still they could not be identical with the experiences that anyone, oneself or another, had actually had before. For inasmuch as they would succeed one's present experiences, they could not also precede them. To assign to one and the same event two different places in the same time order is self-contradictory.

"Thus the reason why the past cannot be recaptured is just that nothing is allowed to count as our recapturing it. It is a necessary fact that if one occupies the position in time that one does at any given moment, one does not at that moment also occupy a different position. If one event temporally precedes another, an experience which is strictly simultaneous with the second of these events cannot also be strictly simultaneous with the first..."

That seemed to provide a lead for my essay. Up till then, it seemed to me that by emphasising *identical* events, Ayer was sliding past the issue: unless he was also invisible, a time traveller who did nothing but stand still and look would change the past just by being there. The question science fiction usually asks is whether there would be major changes, enough to alter history as we know it—or, if by doing so one could prevent one's own existence, would that prevent the changes and so set up a cycling paradox? My own feeling was that each time that time travel is invented the travellers do change the past, so preventing their own existence, but the changes and their effect remain frozen in history, like the discontinuities in the layering of the Martian ice-cap (which hadn't then been discovered).

Not much scope for an essay there. But could I, instead, get a discussion out of this question about the same event occurring at two different points in time? I often discussed my ideas and work with Brian Gardiner, afterwards a physicist with the British Antarctic Survey and co-discoverer of the hole in the ozone layer, and over meals in Glasgow University Union that week we thrashed out the basic scenario of "The Day and the Hour", in terms of a battle between the Patricians and the Plebs, as Brian named the two sides. For the essay they became more prosaically 'Army A' and 'Army B'. The argument was that the explosion which destroys the tank, before a second shell can be fired, does in a sense occur at two different times an hour apart: since no more shells come back from the future, for the winning side the explosion has 'already' happened an hour before they witness it. Whether or not such a thing would ever be possible, it isn't meaningless to imagine it. (My tutor was not impressed.)

After graduating, I spent the winter of 1968 in Somerset with my friends Charles Muir (see Notes to 'In the Arctic, Out of Time') and John Braithwaite, who had been working for Avimo Ltd. on a combined electronic/optical gunsight for the Chieftain Mark VII tank, then the most advanced in the world. John was intrigued by the story and at one point we were going to collaborate on it: he even made a start, setting it in an imaginary Central European state, but abandoned it after a few pages as too Ruritanian. He did supply with me with data on the Chieftain, though actually for the Chieftain Mark IV to protect his security clearance, and I used them in the first version of the story a year or so later.

Having decided to set the story after World War Three, I was intrigued to discover the possibilities for humour. Trelawny, for instance ("We shouldn't have shot him") was Sir Jonathon Trelawny, 1650-1721, commemorated by R.S. Hawker for his stand against James II and imprisonment in the Tower of London:

> "And shall Trelawny live,
> And shall Trelawny die,
> Here's twenty thousand Cornishmen
> Will know the reason why."

A contemporary joke was the reference to tolls on the

Forth Road Bridge, a recent controversy as the first imposition of charges on British roads for many years. As John Watt was singing in 'Fife's Got Everything':

> *'The new Forth Road Bridge, the finest in the country:*
> *A half-a-crown to cross it, we think it's bloody dear;*
> *A bob to cross the Mersey? "Stick it up your jersey!"*
> *Would they pay it down in London? "No bloody fear!"'*

In March of '68, the Clutha folk group had organised a weekend out at Whistlefield. During a not-entirely-sober 21-a-side 'Glasgow versus the rest' football match on Sunday lunchtime (in light but persistent rain), the game was interrupted by a hail from the loch. The late Mick Broderick of the Whistlebinkies was standing up in a boat, framed by the hills behind him, crying "The prince is coming!" Mick later incorporated the phrase into a monologue, describing the increasingly drunken travels of a Highlander spreading the news.

The details on the Highland regiments came from my father, who began World War 2 in the Cameronians before transferring to the Seaforth Highlanders and rising to Captain. He also supplied some basic military background, though for the 'British People's Army' I changed the terminology to match the organisation of the Soviet forces, in which a brigade was the counterpart of a British army division. (The two bombs bracketing Glasgow were of course targeted on the Polaris submarine base in the Holy Loch, and the NATO nuclear weapons store at Glen Douglas.)

The first incarnation of the story drew a blank in the USA and at that time there was no market for short SF in the UK, though James Campbell printed the story in his fanzine *Celtic Warrior*, 1976, illustrated by Gavin Roberts, drawing praise from Ethel Lindsay in *Scottische*. To find out why it wasn't being published, I took it to the UK Milford writers' workshop, where it emerged that I was assuming too much knowledge of the Scottish background for non-Scots to understand it. Comments by Ken Bulmer and Dave Langford were particularly helpful. However, I didn't act on them at the time because I was concentrating on non-fiction.

In 1984, I was lecturing in California at the behest of the Venture Sciences Association. The organisers went bankrupt during the event, and the Treasurer had never paid for my plane ticket, leaving me stranded. I raised the fare home by selling copies of my book "Man and the Planets" at the World Science Fiction Convention, but I was stuck for a further three weeks because I hadn't realised how long it took to clear cheques in California. However, I had met Rick Foss, speakers organiser for the Los Angeles Science Fiction Society, and I gave them a talk at which I sold enough further copies to go home via Cape Canaveral, seeing the October launch of the Space Shuttle *Challenger*.

Immediately after the talk I was buttonholed by Jerry Pournelle, who invited me up to visit Larry and Fuzzy Niven. Jerry afterwards wrote of this evening, "we consumed immense quantities of single malt scotch whiskey and discussed the universe, from the birth of stars to psychic experiences. It was an evening I will not forget, and one I hope some day to repeat." We also discussed a revised version of 'The Day and the Hour', which he and John F. Carr afterwards published in volume V of their anthology series "There Will Be War".

Even when I took the story to Milford-on-Sea, the Chieftain Mk. IV data was well out of date, and for the new version Chris Boyce of the *Glasgow Herald* dug out the data I needed on the Challenger tank. At Jim Campbell's suggestion, I included another contemporary joke harking back to my time in California, to the worst movie I had ever seen—a favourite of Ronald Reagan and Robert McNamara, which I watched in disbelief among a redneck audience leaping up to shake their fists at the screen and shout "Get the goddamm commies!" Although in context *Dheargh Mhatan* seems to mean 'Blue Section', it is actually one of the possible Gaelic translations of "Red Dawn".

Sydney Jordan

In the Arctic, Out of Time

"**T**wo ships coming around the headland, sir."

More straightened to look. "These waters are becoming as busy as the English Channel, Bo'sun. What d'you make of them?"

"Can't tell much from here, sir—but we haven't seen them before."

"Pass the word to the Captain, then." More went aft, and turned a telescope on the newcomers. They had seen the squadron: men were scrambling up the rigging to shorten sail.

The Captain joined him at the rail. "What's this, Mr. More?"

"Two brigs, sir, flying the American flag. They've seen us all right." More passed him the instrument.

The first mate was waiting for orders. "Any signal, sir?"

"I don't think so. They're putting in to join us." The Captain closed the telescope. "Get a reception party organised—and tidy up some of that deck cargo for'ard!" On deck and aloft, the *Resolute* was far from the usual neatness of a Queen's ship. Deck cargo of casks, sledges, ice-triangles and ice-saws; powerful rigging and ice blocks, to cope with the Arctic storms—but at the sight of another flag, even in mid-exploration, the impulse to improve her appearance was automatic.

The American ships dropped anchor a mile away, and a boat put out for the British squadron minutes later. The Captain and More took up their position at the ship's side as it approached.

"Shall we pipe, sir?" asked the Bo'sun.

"I think not, Brown." Both men in the stern of the boat seemed civilians, though in cold-weather gear it was hard to tell. By his awkwardness coming aboard, the older man wasn't even a seaman.

"Dr. Elisha Kane, sir, of the brig *Advance*," said the first American, advancing with hand outstretched. "May I present Dr. Howard Hayes, of the Boston Geographical Society."

"Captain Horatio Austin, H.M.S. *Resolute*, at your service," the Captain said formally. "My first lieutenant, Mr. More. Will you come below, gentlemen?"

In Austin's cabin, as they shed their fur suits and canvas jackets, the Captain called for hot drinks. "It's an unexpected pleasure to meet other ships here," he said. "Though this year, it's less unusual. We overtook Captain Penny's ships earlier this week, and two days ago we sighted another vessel in the Strait."

"No doubt that was the *Prince Albert*, financed by Lady Franklin," said Kane. "She spoke the *Advance* yesterday. They've been searching Barrow Strait and Wellington Channel, but without success, alas."

"Captain Penny's ships were likewise equipped by Lady Franklin," More told him. "She remains convinced of her husband's survival."

"Lady Franklin's misfortune has aroused a great deal of sympathy in the United States," said Kane. "Our two ships, the *Advance* and the *Rescue*, were fitted out by Mr. Henry Grinnell to search for Franklin's party. Has nothing been found?"

"We've found their first winter quarters," said Austin. "It's only a matter of time, now, before their fate is discovered. I've despatched two of my ships, the *Assistance* and *Intrepid*, in the direction of Cape Riley, and that's one of the last possibilities in this area. But after five years, I fear hope must be abandoned. Some survivors of the expedition might have found shelter with the Esquimaux to the south; but if so, word of them should have reached civilisation by now."

"And is this the view of the Admiralty in England?"

"Not officially, of course," said Austin. "But my orders are first to establish whether or not a passage to the west exists along Barrow Strait from Lancaster Sound, *at the same time* searching for traces of Sir John Franklin's expedition. We hope to be back in England by October 1851."

"I see," said Hayes. "Captain, it's possible you could do us a very great service. May I ask you first to look over these papers."

He produced three documents and passed them to Austin. More saw only the seal. The Captain read them through. "I am asked to extend every assistance to your party, Doctor. Though a ship of Her Majesty's Navy is not bound to comply, a request from so high in the United States' administration must almost be received as a command."

"I wouldn't have you feel under any duress, Captain. But I would be very grateful if my daughters and I may transfer to your ships, to continue our work through the winter."

At the word 'daughters' the Captain's expression changed sharply. "A winter in the ice-pack, sir—surely no place for young ladies, especially on a naval vessel. Without appearing inhospitable, let me urge you to take your party south and continue your research in another season."

Hayes was apologetic. "That might seem to be best—but Commander De Haven fears, from the climatic conditions, that his ships may be caught in the 'middle ice' of Baffin Bay. They are not equipped for wintering in the ice, and conditions aboard would be at least unpleasant, at worst hazardous."

"Extremely so, if the hulls were to be nipped," Austin agreed. "I shall review our position as regards stores and equipment, Doctor, and let you have my decision within the hour. Please call my steward if you require anything. Mr. More, come with me, please."

A midshipman was despatched to fetch the chief quarter-master. "This is a fine situation," said the Captain. "The fellow must know their President, or even be related to him, to judge from those letters! I can't risk a diplomatic incident, not when those ships have been sent by a philanthropist to search for Franklin. We can't refuse to take their passengers, if there's a chance they won't get through Baffin Bay before the ice closes in."

"If they're not prepared for the winter, they'd have scurvy to contend with," More agreed.

"And if the ships are crushed, they'll be lucky to survive at all unless they reach a whaling station," Austin went on. "Imagine the outcry if we refused and these young women perished!"

However reluctantly, Austin had to take the American scientists aboard. The *Resolute* had a tier of cabins on each side, for her unusually large complement of officers; it was arranged that More would share with the third lieutenant, so putting his own cabin and the third's at the Americans' disposal when the second lieutenant, McLintock, moved to the other side. By the time their gear was moved next day, the scientists and their equipment were on their way across.

Dr. Hayes came aboard first, to supervise the hoisting of wooden boxes marked 'Instruments - with Care'. Then the girls came up the side, each followed by an American sailor in case of accident. Despite the cold wind, they both threw back their fur hoods to be introduced to the Captain. More was struck immediately by the contrast in their looks: the taller one was blonde, almost Scandinavian in appearance, while the other's hair was wavy and jet black. Her height was little over five feet. Perhaps they're only half-sisters, More thought as the remaining dunnage was hoisted to the deck. The older girl put up her hood again almost at once, though Austin was inviting his guests to come below; but the other, still bare-headed, took an appraising look round before she followed. Her eyes met More's and stopped—just for a second, but he felt his insides turn to water. Without resuming her survey of the deck, she turned and followed the others aft.

To his satisfaction, More recollected himself a second before the American officer at his side. As More's eye lit on him, he too clicked back to reality. "There's one thing I can say, sir," he said, turning to the ship's side. "I am purely sorry not to see the effect that young lady will have on Her Majesty's Navy!" And with that he was gone, following the sailors into the boat; leaving More to look after him, in turn, trying to extrapolate from that parting shot.

Near mid-day, the *Resolute's* search parties returned from the shore. Penny's ships had gone on, intending to make another landing further along the coast; *Pioneer* already had steam up. To save time Austin ordered the tender to tow *Resolute* into the main channel, crews lining the decks for the customary three cheers as they passed Grinnell's two ships. The two girls appeared briefly aft to wave handkerchiefs, but the cold had driven them below long before the *Resolute* made sail.

Progress along the Strait was slow; the wind was freshening, and beginning to turn against them. Penny's ships were still ahead when More was relieved, and with great relief went below. The weather, he foresaw, would be thoroughly nasty by nightfall. He left his heavy jacket and gloves in his new cabin, and set off to claim the hot tea that should be waiting. At the change of watch, as ice thawed from clothing and boots and kettles boiled on all sides, the ship filled with fog below decks; and out of it, there came an astonishing apparition.

Though the girls had come aboard in long skirts, cold-weather gear had hidden their femininity. Below decks, however, warm air was distributed mechanically. The dark girl was now wearing sailor's shirt and trousers, but the effect was anything but masculine.

"Oh, come on, Lieutenant!" she said brightly, before he found words. "It can't be *that* long since you left England, surely?"

"Young ladies don't dress like that in England," said More, swallowing hard.

She dropped him a curtsey—and he'd never seen that done in trousers before. "Why, thank you, sir! I'm glad you approve."

Naval officers are not fools—not even when facing astonishing young women, instead of fire and storm. More could almost hear her saying, "But Captain, Lieutenant More said it was all right."

"No miss," he said firmly, "your clothes would cause a stir there."

"No doubt," she said casually. "When we reach England, I shall have to be demure and conventional. But for a winter in the ice, I must dress practically, don't you agree?"

"I don't think it'll be necessary to go to these lengths, miss."

"I have a feeling I'll surprise you, Lieutenant," she said with disconcerting firmness. "I've come to the Arctic to work, to conduct a serious scientific investigation, not to be decorative at the Captain's table. Right now for instance I'm going to make friends with the crew, and I want them to accept me as an equal, not as some fashionable lady amusing herself. Excuse me?"

That did catch More unprepared. The Americans were obviously under the Captain's authority on the *Resolute*—but could More place the fo'c'sle out of bounds to them without referring to Austin? Probably not. He let her go, unable to resist staring after her, then made at once for the Captain's cabin.

❧

There were no immediate repercussions from the girl's trip for'ard, though neither More nor Austin could imagine the effect of her arrival. Austin felt that he couldn't restrict his guests' movements until something did happen—probably an embarrassed deputation of seamen, asking for Miss Hayes's visits to be stopped. That rough masculine environment was all Jack could call his own at sea, and he would fight to preserve it. But nothing did happen, and More found himself burning with curiosity. Could she really have pulled it off, and been 'accepted as an equal'? Of course it was unthinkable to ask.

The gale continued all next day, keeping the passengers below deck where everyone would like to be. Little progress was made through the ice, although *Pioneer* took the *Resolute* in tow. The gale was too fierce for gunpowder or ice-saws to be used, and to work the two ships round bergs *Pioneer* often had to make the *Resolute* cannon off the sides of the lead. So late in the season, these delays could make the difference between success and failure: the further *Resolute* penetrated before she was frozen in, the less old ice she would have to negotiate next summer to reach the western sea. Opinion at the Admiralty was known to be turning against the search for the North-West Passage, which had apparently claimed Franklin's two ships with all hands. Other lives had been lost on costly searching expeditions, and still no-one had got through the Passage either way.

Next morning there were signs of a change, and by midday they were clear of the pack. Both Austin and More were on deck when the bosun's whistle sent the men scrambling aloft. One figure heading for the upper fore topsail looked strangely small—but before More caught on fully, the Captain's bellow rang across the deck.

"Bo'sun, have that young woman brought down from the mast—and escort her aft, to me!"

Everything stopped. In the general scramble to the yards, few if any of the crew had realised the girl was with them. They hung staring in the shrouds as the girl returned to the deck, without help from the seaman ordered across to her. She walked aft proudly ahead of Brown, hair whipping under her cap. Another roared order set the men scrambling again to make sail.

Austin was head and shoulders taller than the girl, but she was in no way intimidated. Her eyes were bright, and a smile was threatening to break out. She had wanted to see how far she could go, and now she was looking forward to an argument; but Austin gave her no chance to make a speech.

"Miss Hayes, in your visits to the fo'c'sle, have you made the acquaintance of the sailmaker, Thomas Kelly?"

It wasn't the opening she'd expected. "Old Tom?—Why yes. He's a sweet old fellow."

One point back to her, thought More, mentally keeping score

without taking his eyes off the work aloft. But it wasn't enough to stop the Captain. "Ahem! quite so. Then on your next visit there, having first of course obtained the permission of the captain of the forecastle, please give Mr. Kelly my compliments and ask him to sing *Farewell Nancy*. I don't doubt that the song is in his repertoire."

Her baffled pause must have lasted a good two seconds. "Er—yes, Captain. Thank you." She went below, and More could return his attention to the deck at last.

"Nicely done, sir, if I may say so."

"I thought it wasn't bad, Mr. More. Curiosity will drive her to it, I imagine, and the hint may be more effective than a direct order. God, I always knew American women were emancipated, but that one thinks she's fully the equal of a man!"

"Her upbringing must have been extraordinary," More agreed. "Even in the United States, I can't imagine her behaviour being accepted at any level of society."

"And yet she's a highly educated young woman," said the Captain. "To have mastered the sciences so thoroughly, of course, she's had to have private tuition, mostly from her father; but to be capable of absorbing it, she must have been at the best of schools beforehand. Quite a number of them, I imagine," he added drily.

Although it was mid-day, the sun was low in the sky. Ice-bows surrounded it, and the 'blink' of ice was noticeable on the horizon. The isolated bergs in the channel were becoming more numerous, beginning to take on the appearance of a pack once again.

Kelly was singing *Saint James's Hospital* when the girl came into the fo'c'sle. She tried to join the listeners unnoticed, but someone coughed loudly and an embarrassed silence fell.

"Oh, don't stop just because I come in," she said.

Kelly looked down at his feet. "That's not a fit song for you to hear, miss."

She grinned. "Try me! It's a lovely song. There's an American version, did you know?"

"The Cap'n'd have the skin off my back, miss Diana, if he heard I'd offended your ears with it."

A seaman gave up his place, and was rewarded with a radiant smile as she slipped into the circle. "Oh, but he told me to ask you. The Captain wants you to sing for me."

Kelly smiled. "I can hardly believe that, miss."

"He did too! Just after I went up the foremast this morning. I thought he would raise Cain about that, but all he told me was to ask for this song. *Farewell Nancy*—is that right?"

"I see," said Kelly, not at all pleased.

"Don't you know it?"

"Why yes, miss, it's sold as a broadside at home, and very popular."

"Come on, then."

"Well, I think the Captain was just having his little joke, miss," Kelly said hopefully.

"Oh no," Diana assured him. "It was the last thing in the world I expected him to say, but it wasn't any joke. 'Give Mr. Kelly my compliments, and ask him to sing *Farewell Nancy*.' I didn't even know you sang—I haven't heard a note of music since I came aboard this ship."

"Better you never had, miss, if it was left up to me," Kelly said heavily. "Give me a note on the accordion, Bill." He cleared his throat.

"*'Fare you well, my dearest Nancy, for now I must leave you,*
All across the western ocean I am bound for to go;
Don't let me long voyage to trouble and grieve you,
For I will return in the spring as you know.'

"Then she says:

'Like a little seaboy I'll dress and go with you,
In the midst of all dangers your help I'll remain.
In the cold stormy weather when the winds are a-blowin',

My dear I'll be ready to reef your topsail.'

"I think, miss, this verse would be the one the Captain wanted you to hear...

" 'Well your pretty slender fingers couldn't handle our tackle,

Your delicate feet to our topmast can't go,

And your little behind, love, would freeze in the wind, love -

I would have you at home when the stormy winds do blow."

"I see," she murmured. She heard the song out to the end, and praised Kelly's singing. "Are there many songs about girls dressing up as sailors and going to sea?"

"Yes, miss; it's a common dream of lads on long trips, I suppose. But the Captain wouldn't suggest you heard *Short Jacket and White Trousers*, or *The Handsome Cabin Boy*, for instance."

"Why not, Tom? You can tell me, I won't take offense."

"Well, you see, in those songs the Captain himself fancies the young girl concerned; and in one of them, well, he acts on it, y'see."

There were grins from the crew and Kelly would have changed the subject; but Diana gave him a wicked smile, drawing up her knees and hugging them. "Sing me that!" she demanded.

More was on watch next day when the girls came on deck. It was the first time he had seen them attempt any naturalistic work, though that morning Dr. Hayes had towed a small net over the side for an hour, bringing up a surprising number of marine organisms. The girls seemed mainly interested in the few sea birds still following the ship; watching them through a glass they made a few sketches, and tried to lure some with scraps of bread. But Diana seemed to grow bored, and came to tackle More.

"Why don't you let the men sing at work?"

Taken aback once again! "Pardon, miss?"

"I asked Tom Kelly to sing for me last night, as the Captain suggested. Don't act surprised, lieutenant, I bet you didn't miss a word of that conversation! But old Tom told me you don't allow singing on deck, not that anyone would want to in this weather."

"That's quite true," said More. "Queen's Regulations, miss, I'm afraid."

"Mean regulations, if you ask me," she went on. "You can't call the songs 'forebitters' if they're not allowed to sing on the forebitts. I want to register a protest!"

"It'll go at the very head of my report," More promised, amused. The coming winter certainly wasn't going to be dull—if they could keep her from tearing the whole ship apart!

"Yeah, I bet. But what about those fabulous work songs we had on our ships—the hauling shanties, capstan shanties and the rest? They're not exactly fun, unless you're listening to them, but they help the work along."

"I dare say they do, miss, but this is a naval vessel. We set rhythms for hauling with the bosun's whistle, as I'm sure you've heard. It's not for us to argue with Q.R.'s."

"Yah, the Queen's a meanie." She stuck out her tongue and wandered back to the rail. When she got to England, More realised, she might well be presented at court. He hoped he'd be there to see that. The older girl, Evelyn, had been listening to their conversation with an ambiguous smile. More suspected her of playing a part: she was always demure, taking the air on deck on father's arm, but he thought she was capable of the same antics as her sister. She expected Diana to get her fingers burned, and she'd be amused by it, if it wasn't too serious.

The wind was still unfavourable and progress was slow. Just after noon a brilliant series of parhelia and halos formed around the sun, and More despatched a midshipman to inform the Americans. Two orange halos encircled the true sun, the larger one intersected by a prismatic halo surrounding the zenith. Parallel to the horizon, four parhelia appeared in the vertical halos; belts of orange connected them to the true sun, and another ran down to a deep orange mass on the horizon. On the sides away from the sun, the parhelia were elongated into cones of prismatic colours.

"That's a sign of cold weather," More remarked to Diana, who happened to be nearest him. "As one of the seaman put it, 'When them 'ere sun dogs shows themselves we always gets double allowance from Jack Frost.'"

"The ice is certainly getting thicker," she replied. The *Resolute* was still making progress under sail, but course changes were more and more frequent.

"*Pioneer* will have to tow us soon," said More. "We shan't get much further, I believe—there's 'ice blink' all along the horizon ahead."

"Yeah, that's no water sky," she said, making him feel rather foolish: with her enquiring mind, she'd have learned to read the Arctic sky on the *Advance*. She had put on a curious pair of darkened spectacles, which she now handed to him. "Try these, Lieutenant, the effect's much more noticeable."

The glasses made an astonishing difference. Unlike the smoked ones and veils used by the Navy, they cut out eyestrain without otherwise limiting vision. "That's amazing," said More. "How's it done?"

"It's a special glass," said Diana. "It eliminates the glare, which is caused by light scattered from the ice."

"We've got to hand it to you Americans for ingenuity," said More. "There wouldn't be much risk of snow blindness using these. Another good idea we'll hear nothing more about, I suppose— what the devil's that?"

"What?" she asked. Without the glasses, she was now at a disadvantage.

"A dark speck, over there. It'll be directly below the sun in a moment, it's just entering the orange column. Dr. Hayes, sir, can you see it?"

"I can indeed, sir." The scientist had whipped out a small

telescope. "It's too far off to make out—but it's no bird, I'll swear to that!"

"Listen!" said Diana. A low sound, like continuous distant thunder, was rolling over the ship.

"Icebergs breaking off some glacier?" More suggested weakly.

Everyone on deck was staring now, as the speck moved steadily across their bows. "It's twelve degrees above the horizon," announced Barnes, the third lieutenant. When the mystery appeared, he had been measuring the separations of the parhelia for the log.

"I never heard a mirage make a sound before, sir," said the man at the wheel, nervously. Sailors were superstitious, even in the middle of the nineteenth century.

The speck passed on, and was lost behind the islands on their starboard bow. The sound faded, and More looked hopefully to Hayes for some explanation.

"Fascinating," said the American. He seemed strangely excited. "Fascinating."

"Could you advance any hypothesis, sir, as to what that was we saw?"

Hayes pulled himself together. "No, sir, I have nothing to suggest. If we could believe our eyes, we should have to say: a flying machine, travelling north, perhaps to the Pole itself. But obviously that's impossible; quite impossible, gentlemen." But he was still intensely excited, and almost at once he went below.

As the seaman had predicted, the day grew colder as it wore on. Young ice formed over the sea as soon as darkness fell. The night was bitter, the stars overhead so brilliant that it seemed unfair they gave no warmth. Next morning ice met the eye in all directions; the ships continued to make progress along the few clear lanes remaining, but soon after midday a chill fog reached out across the channel. Frost formed on the shrouds and deck fittings as the *Resolute* crept on, taking soundings with increasing frequency. When they anchored the ships to the ice at nightfall, it was estimated that they were in the lee of Griffith's Island, sighted ahead in the forenoon.

There had been another strange episode during the day, however. The Hayes party had come on deck in mid-afternoon, and remained for some time despite the biting chill—almost, More thought afterwards, as if they were waiting for something. They had been on deck for nearly an hour when another strange sound came to their ears.

"That can't be the beat of *Pioneer*'s screws, surely," said Barnes, his head cocked to the side.

"If it were, she'd be bearing down on us at an incredible speed," said More. The fog made it impossible to place the mechanical throbbing, but it was growing swiftly in volume. "Sound the foghorn, there—and the bell, continuously!"

The noise doubled and redoubled, till the open air was like an engine-room. People looked in all directions, wildly, and Barnes was first to see the thing when it appeared.

It was only a shadow in the mist, shapeless, though More had the impression of some beating or revolving airfoil. Beneath it a beam of light shone, like a single ray of sunshine. It came from astern, from roughly where *Pioneer* should be, and passed the *Resolute*'s port side, turning north across her bows. In a moment it had vanished, and the deafening noise was soon muffled by the fog.

If yesterday's phenomenon had excited the Americans, today's stimulated them beyond speech. Looking round for their comments More saw them disappearing below, leaving him to face the bewildered stares of the crew.

He had to show the ship's officers were not alarmed. "It seems there's another mystery in these waters, besides the disappearance of Sir John Franklin," he remarked, as outwardly calm as Austin would have been.

"You don't think—they might be connected, sir?" the helmsman ventured.

"We've no reason to think so at present," said More, with a firmness which wasn't entirely genuine. "But if there is a connection, Her Majesty's Navy will get to the bottom of it. Mr. Jones!" The midshipman, who was listening with awed respect, snapped to alertness. "You saw as much as we did, I suppose? Report it to the Captain, if you please. *If he asks*, say that in my opinion he's not required on deck meantime. If anything more occurs, of course we will inform him."

But nothing more did happen, up to the time the *Resolute* found solid ice ahead. *Pioneer* was somewhere astern, out of hailing distance. The fog was still spread over the ships next day, and since they had a firm anchorage on the edge of the floe Austin decided not to move. The pack ice was closing in, impelled by wind and tides further up the channel. Throughout the day the pack grew more compressed, and the hull began to creak and stir uneasily as it took the pressure. Though the *Resolute*'s hull was doubled with wood, the bow and stern made to resemble the ends of a caisson with alternate layers of wood and iron, everyone wondered uneasily if she would in fact withstand the strain. By nightfall, however, there was still no danger.

Jones and Middleton, the two midshipmen, were playing cards down in their berth. Near the waterline the grinding noises from the ice were louder, so they didn't hear Diana's approach.

"May I join you, boys?"

Both leaped to their feet. "Miss Diana! we didn't...that is..."

"Now don't get uptight," she said, whatever that odd expression might mean. "I just wondered what you two were doing down here, when the ship's anchored."

"There's very little to do, miss," Jones agreed. "Unless the officers invite us for cards or conversation, we're left to our own devices down here. There's always studying to be done, of course, but too much reading strains the eyes."

"You haven't much light for reading," she agreed, eyeing the cards. "What did I interrupt—millions of dollars changing hands here?"

"Er—not exactly, miss. We *were* playing for coppers, just to make it more interesting."

"That's good, I might just about be able to raise the stake then." She moved nearer to the sea-chest serving as a table. "Deal me in?"

Diana won the first game, very easily. "You let me win out of politeness!" she accused. They were both in their mid-teens, and their blushes gave them away. She kidded them unmercifully, until their only defence was to play properly. Half-an-hour later, she had lost four games in a row and discovered she had no more change.

"Well, you'll have to trust me, gentlemen. If I don't regain my fortune in the next few hands, I'll have to settle up with you tomorrow."

"Oh, that's no good, miss Diana," said Jones. He'd had his daily rum ration not long before she joined them, and in the stuffy 'tweendecks atmosphere it had gone a little to his head—along with the excitement of the game and the general effect of Diana's company. "Debts have to be settled on the spot, here."

"Then you must give me a chance to win something back," she said, laughing. "I can't pay!"

"If you can't pay up, we must each have a kiss," said Jones, greatly daring. "Don't you agree, Middleton?"

Diana looked at him coyly, from under her long lashes. "I fear, sir, my kisses are not won so easily."

"We'll see about that," cried Jones, carried away. "Catch her, Middleton!"

"Oh no you don't!" A laughing scuffle ensued. Middleton found it surprisingly hard to catch her by the arms: the thought occurred to him that she might even know how to fight in earnest.

"What the devil is this?" Brown, who was responsible for discipline below decks, loomed over them. The cane grasped in his hand gave his authority some emphasis.

Jones scrambled to his feet, suddenly sobered. "Just a friendly game of cards, sir," he offered. It sounded weak.

"Cards!" snorted the bo'sun. "Cards are very well, gentlemen, but they don't let you turn the ship into a bear-garden. Anything else to say? Middleton?"

"Nothing, sir." They both knew what was coming.

"Then, gentlemen, I'll trouble you to bend. Leave us, miss Hayes, if you please."

"There's no need for this!" Diana protested. "It was just a friendly game, even if it got a little out of hand. Maybe that was my fault."

"I don't doubt that it was, miss. I trust you will take note of the outcome."

"If you punish them, in that case, you should cane me too!"

"It may come to that in future, miss, with the Captain's authority," Brown said grimly. "I know he has asked you, more than once, to dress and act as befits a lady of your station. If you prefer to dress like the boys and lead them into mischief, you may well share their punishment in future. Mr. Jones, step forward!"

Word of Brown's threat went round the ship like wildfire. There was, indeed, an erotic rumour that it had been carried out, and that the girl admired her bruises before a mirror night and morning. More was displeased to find himself stirred by it; though not more so, probably, than any other man aboard. Most of the crew would have liked nothing better than a chance to check the story. The danger, or possibly some guilt for Middleton and Jones, kept her from actively disturbing the ship for a few days, though her voice and manner remained provocative; but a more serious incident was to subdue her still further.

Austin had waited throughout the next morning for a show-down with Dr. Hayes. Nothing happened, which was a little disconcerting; but Austin was not easily put off. When the afternoon watch produced no request for an interview, Austin took the initiative and had the scientist summoned to his cabin.

"I've been expecting to hear from you, Dr. Hayes, concerning last night's disciplinary action."

"There didn't seem to be any occasion for that, sir. Hopefully, Diana has learned her lesson. I know she has been a trial to you since we came aboard."

"Good God, man, can't you control your own daughter?"

Hayes shrugged helplessly. "She lacks a mother's influence." He seemed to find the idea almost funny.

"Dr. Hayes, I have been very patient with these disturbances to the ship's routine, but now they must stop. Brown is responsible for order below decks. Your daughter put him in an impossible position, and he took the only conceivable action."

"Oh, I agree, Captain. I think your bo'sun handled the situation very well. Diana's a law unto herself, but this experience should teach her some restraint. I don't think she's fully appreciated, until now, what it is to be aboard a naval vessel; I'm only glad she wasn't responsible for any more serious breach of discipline."

"So am I, sir, very glad indeed. Let me remind you that we face a full winter in darkness, trapped in the ice of this channel. If your daughter's behaviour were to provoke an assault on her, that would be a hanging matter. Even if I considered the men concerned had been led on, as those boys were last night, I would have no alternative. I expect you to ensure, Doctor, that no such incident occurs. Good day, sir!"

An icy gale arose, clearing away the mist. It showed the *Resolute* completely surrounded by ice, about a mile from shore, with *Pioneer* about the same distance off to the east. It began to look as if the ships were fast for the winter, as the ice grew still more compacted under the thrust of the wind and pressure ridges began to rise around them. The hull continued to resist the ice, and Lieut. McLintock was seen checking his sledges and equipment. Austin waited for the ice to settle more firmly; and on the second day he had another breach of discipline to contend with.

The seaman gave his name as 'Jenkins'. Somehow, as he questioned the man, More formed the idea that the name might be an alias. He had been found searching the Hayes party's cabin, and refused to give any explanation or say anything in his defence. When he was brought before the Captain, his attitude was the same.

"A final chance, Jenkins," Austin said at last. "Have you nothing at all to say before I pass sentence?"

"No, sir." The man seemed quite indifferent to the proceedings. He was tall, with a noticeable sun-tan and a surprisingly smooth face for a seaman. More had noticed him many times during the voyage, for his evident laziness as well as his height: he often came in for the rough edge of Brown's tongue, and probably on occasion for his boot.

"Very well. Two dozen lashes for attempted theft—and another dozen for dumb insolence. March him out!" As the door closed behind prisoner and escort, Austin turned to his first lieutenant. He was extremely displeased.

"It's my belief, Mr. More, that this will be the first flogging ever to be conducted in the search for the North-West Passage—probably the first within hundreds of miles of this latitude. A distinction I am most reluctant to claim for any ship or party under my command. I might further add, this is at most the fifth or sixth such punishment I have had to order since I gained my first command, and certainly the first on any of my voyages of exploration." All this was certainly true. Austin was one of the most celebrated naval explorers of the century, and well known as a firm but humane Captain. There were hundreds of volunteers from the fleet whenever he was preparing an expedition. All the *Resolute's* crew were volunteers, and many of them, Brown for example, had sailed under him on previous voyages.

"Any comments, Mr. More?"

"Very few, sir. Jenkins is one of five men we took on at

Plymouth, on our way down the Channel. His references were good, though he's never been to the Arctic before. Apparently he and his friends aren't much liked, however: they keep pretty much to themselves, off-watch."

Austin folded his hands on the table-top. "I don't like this, Mr. More. This has not been a happy voyage, even before the Americans came aboard. The regrettable differences between Lieutenant McLintock and myself have tended to promote rivalries among the crew. While that stress will be removed once McLintock is on his way, we will then be left shorthanded. Unfortunately *Assistance* and *Intrepid* have not rejoined us before the ice closed in, so we may have to wait until next spring to balance up the crews. Meantime, I have here Lieutenant McLintock's provisional selections for the sledge parties; and I note that none of the Plymouth clique are among them. I'd like to separate them, Mr. More. I don't suppose I can *order* McLintock to take them; he couldn't refuse, but it would be bad for morale, and make it obvious that we see these men as a threat."

Austin looked up. "I'll leave this in your hands for the moment, Mr. More. Find out if any of them volunteered for the search parties; if not, see if any of them can be induced to do so; and if they can, try to persuade Lieutenant McLintock to include them."

More left the cabin, wondering how far this incident would go in its consequences. Already, with the grim ritual of a flogging ahead, it was a cloud 'bigger than a man's hand.' Austin hadn't needed to state the possibility he saw in the coming night: that his ship might gain the further distinction of the first Arctic mutiny.

The Americans kept to their quarters during the punishment, but the incident finally brought home to Diana the severity of the discipline she had been upsetting. She resumed the same modest costume as her sister, and kept to the after part of the ship.

Beyond doubt, the *Resolute* was fixed in the ice for the winter.

By the time the gale blew itself out, great pressure ridges twenty feet or more in height were thrusting up out of the pack, especially between the ships and Griffith's Island. Only the tips of *Pioneer's* masts could be seen, and parties crossing from ship to ship detoured to avoid treacherous footing. The sledges were unloaded and trial runs were made, as McLintock's party prepared for departure.

Diana Hayes was on deck with More and the Captain, when McLintock came up with a fistful of papers. "These are my requisitions for the journey, sir. I'd be obliged if you'd grant them your formal approval."

"H'm. Clothing list per man: one inside flannel, one serge frock, one duck jumper, one pair of drawers, one pair of breeches, one Welsh wig.. I'll have to go through all this at length, Mr. McLintock. Come below, please. Excuse me, miss Hayes."

"There's something between those two, isn't there?" Diana remarked, as they disappeared into the hatchway.

"Pointless to deny it," More agreed. "Inevitable, really, when you consider it. Captain Austin is one of the last great naval explorers: the world's so well known these days, the search for the North-West Passage is probably the last challenge apart from the Poles themselves. McLintock's likewise the acknowledged master of sledge exploration, since his search for Franklin south of Barrow Strait, and he's out to prove that the North-West Passage is penetrable by sledge. He sees a future of trading camps along the Strait, like coaching stations. Naturally he sees Captain Austin as a rival, looking for a sea passage, and it's believed in the Fleet that this expedition will prove one or other of them to be right."

"I see. So McLintock's going on, to reach the far end of the Passage before all daylight goes?"

"That's right. If they get through they'll rendezvous with McLure's *Investigator*, somewhere beyond Melville Island, and return to us in the spring. I don't say the Captain hopes they'll turn back, but it'll be a triumph for him if *he's* the first man through the Passage, by ship, next year."

"Well, I'll cheer for the Captain," she declared. "Do you think he'll get his triumph, or will the sledges get through first?"

"The signs aren't hopeful," More said sadly. "On the trial runs the sledges have found old ice out beyond the islands, suggesting that the channel remains blocked throughout the summer. If that's the case, we'll be forced to turn back towards Baffin Bay before the end of the season."

"That would be a shame," she said. "I'd like to be the first girl through the North-West Passage...How can you tell that it's old ice out there?"

More was becoming used to her changes of mental direction. "When sea ice forms it's blue and glassy. Often it breaks up into small hummocks in the pack, but it's still no real hindrance to a sledge because of its smoothness. Under summer sunshine it becomes dirty and yellowish, and pools form on its surface, leaving it uneven when it freezes again. The more seasons the ice lasts, the more difficult it becomes to cross."

"So you can tell an ice-floe's history just by looking at it," she mused. "I don't suppose they'd take me with the sledge parties, do you?"

"Oh, too much to hope for," More agreed with feeling.

"The Captain might send you along to look after me," she retorted. Her voice suddenly became unbelievably seductive. "And wouldn't that be nice for both of us?"

More was taken by surprise again. For a second he thought the Arctic wind had stopped blowing. She was standing directly before him, looking up into his eyes. "You look pretty good with ice in your beard," she went on casually, but without shifting her gaze.

"It may look manly, but it irritates the lips a good deal," More managed, unable to believe this was happening.

"Hey, that's too bad," she said sympathetically, managing to make fun of him at the same time—and then she thrust her hands deep into her pockets and spun away from him, off to see the sledge dogs being hoisted over the side.

By nightfall, all was ready for the sledges to set out at first light. Though McLintock believed that the only way through the Passage was over the ice, he was still a naval officer and beyond doubt this was a naval party. Each sledge was named, and officially designated: 'H.M. Sledge *Perseverance, Endeavour, Lady Franklin...*' In tribute to the American passengers, and the New York philanthropist whose ships had brought them, one was duly christened 'H.M. Sledge *Grinnell*', by Evelyn Hayes. Each sledge had its own flag and motto—'One and all', 'Nil desperandum', 'Prospice respice'. More's favourite, for the sledge *Resolute*, read 'St. George and merry England; onward to the rescue'; showing that one officer, at least, still considered himself to be searching primarily for Franklin. The sledges were loaded with tents, sleeping bags, cooking apparatus, guns, instruments...and printed notices to be placed in cairns along the way, giving the position of the ships and the location of food depots. One party, More happened to know, also carried advertising bills for the Margate Steam Packet Company, which should puzzle any wandering Esquimaux or plundering bears. Another detail which appealed to him, in the plan of operations, was the order reading 'The several parties are to understand, that they have the option of leaving behind any portion of their allowance of rum, and that a proper proportion of tea will be given in compensation for it.'

A small party of men, including More and the Captain, went with the sledge parties for the first ten miles along the Strait. Progress was good at first, but slowed when they hit the old, uneven ice beyond the islands. The heavier sledges, drawn by dogs, were able to press on, but those pulled by the men became heavy burdens as soon as their sails were lowered. The experimental kites, intended to lift the prows of the sledges to make progress easier, proved effective at first but were unreliable when the wind became gusty. After two hours hauling and slipping on the difficult hummocks, More was heartily glad when the Captain decided to turn back. The crews exchanged three cheers, and Austin wished the sledge parties God speed; and without any wish to be sharing the journey ahead, those left behind returned to the icebound ships.

With the sledge parties gone, there was unusual freedom of movement on the cramped decks of the *Resolute*. More had a cabin to himself again, a luxury he would certainly welcome during the trying months of the winter. He intended to do some serious reading, though he wouldn't have much free time: he would be heavily involved in activities to make the winter pass quickly—amateur dramatics, concerts, a ship's newspaper...

Snow covered all the islands by late September, and fox tracks were seen on the ice around the ships. Canvas housings like huge tents were put up over the decks; and the lumber was cleared off, to make room for exercise in bad weather.

None of the five men from Plymouth had gone with the sledge parties. McLintock, knowing their bad record and unpopularity, had simply declined to take them, and for Austin to thrust them upon him might be construed as attempted sabotage. For the grim race with winter he had undertaken, McLintock was entitled to willing helpers who would pull their weight. But as the days grew noticeably shorter, and the work to be done grew less, it seemed that the clique obeyed orders and stood watches only because they chose to do so. Another showdown over 'dumb insolence' seemed inevitable; Brown was seen to carry his cane more aggressively, and even on occasion to produce a rope's end.

By November the sun no longer broke the horizon even at midday, and the ships should have been settled into winter routine. Instead there was the feeling of an impending threat, and people tended to look over their shoulders as they went about the ship. Once More came upon the five Plymouth men standing together in a circle, as if listening to voices far away. When he demanded "What's this?" they just stared at him, and walked away.

Something had to be done. Even Diana Hayes seemed uneasy about the disruptive influences working in the ship. Penny's ships were twenty miles away, too far to help if there was trouble. Austin brought men and officers over from *Pioneer*, and ordered the sergeant of marines to keep alert. It seemed impossible for five men to take over the *Resolute* from twenty, but on the other hand, he couldn't place them all in detention without definite cause. The bad old days of the war against Bonaparte were far in the past; and apart from the attempted theft weeks ago, the suspects had committed no open breach of discipline. They paid a great deal of attention to the Hayes party, however; it might just be because two of them were girls, but it was as if the Americans were being shadowed. Each time the watcher was ordered for'ard, his obedience was more indifferent. They seemed to be openly waiting for something to happen; but what *could* happen, so far from civilisation, defied the imagination.

"Something strikes you as funny, Mr. More?"

"I was just wondering, sir, how Lieutenant Osborn will describe these events, when he relays them all to the world."

"Scribbling again, is he?" said Austin. "What's this epic to be called?"

More chuckled. "He's trying to keep it a secret, sir. But 'Stray Leaves from an Arctic Journal' is the title rumoured around."

Austin groaned. "Stray leaves aren't common up here, or leaves of any sort. I don't know where young officers get their literary influences, these days." He picked up a report from the table. "'At 2.00 hours, being still confined to the tents by the gale, we remarked the approach of a bear. We loaded our guns with ball, which we discharged at a range of fifteen yards. We took Bruin in the shoulder, little to his liking evidently, for at once he took to his heels...' Can you imagine how this will be received by my Lords of the Admiralty?"

In daylight, this part of the Arctic had been desolate; but a full silver moon, wheeling around the zenith for several days and nights, cast a new beauty over the scene. Tracks around the ship showed that not all the bears were in hibernation yet. For a few hours around noon the sky filled with colour, ranging from deep rosy red, through every shade of pink and blue, to cold blue-black over the mountains to the north. Early afternoon found More and Brown on deck, checking the accumulation of ice on spars and shrouds. It wasn't a major problem in these waters—annual precipitation was as low as in the Sahara desert—but a routine check had to be made. They started with the spanker boom and worked for'ard, Brown flashing beams from his lantern across the furled canvas overhead. Some aurora was flickering in the sky to the north.

They were moving from the foremast to the bowsprit when the shooting star appeared. A golden fireball, it was bigger and moving more slowly than any meteor More had seen before. It came into being in the north, not far from the horizon, and drew its ruler-straight trail up the sky towards the zenith. Both men sighed involuntarily as it faded, leaving the dispersing trail at rest for a second—then it lit up again, passing over the ship now, bright enough to throw shadows on the deck.

"I never saw that happen before!" More exclaimed, as it was hidden by the fore topgallant. He and Brown started aft to follow it, catching glimpses between the sails as the meteor flared south.

They were already amidships, negotiating the remaining deck cargo, when More realised they were being followed. Someone had come out of the fo'c'sle and was following them aft. "See who that is behind us, Brown!" More ordered, and kept going. He didn't need a lantern to find his way about *Resolute*'s deck, and he kept his eyes on that extraordinary star.

Ahead of him, a hatch shot open. More stopped dead, expecting trouble—he felt matters were coming to a head. But Dr. Hayes and the two girls sprang out. Coming from the light below they didn't see him, but rushed to the stern to watch the meteor. "Look at that!" More heard Diana cry in wonder.

There had been no alarm on deck, no shouting, and the shooting star itself made no sound. How had the Americans known it was there? On an impulse he couldn't justify, More slipped down the hatch into the light. The Hayes's cabin, which had earlier been his own, stood open. More opened up his heavy clothes and stepped inside, closing the door behind him.

This was precisely the offense for which the Plymouth seaman had been flogged, he realised as he drew off his gloves. In the same moment he saw the book, lying open on the table.

The chapter title, printed at the top of the pages, was 'In the Ice'. The three critical passages were printed in italics, so his eye was drawn to them at once. The first two were the *Resolute*'s log entries for the flying machine mirages—and the third, incredibly, for today's date and this very time, read:

"3h.05m.. A strange fireball sighted, coming from the northern sky. It was seen to be extinguished near the zenith, then to reappear as brightly as before further along its track. It proceeded into the southern sky, eventually vanishing behind the islands. All who saw it were impressed with its brilliance and its unusually slow pace across the heavens." The last words had been underlined in red ink.

How in God's name could the log entry for the incident already be printed in *this* book—probably in his own words, since he was Officer of the Watch? Unable to believe his eyes, More flipped to the cover. It had a protective jacket of glossy paper, more shiny than he had ever seen before. The book was "'Voyage to Controversy', by Howard T. Hayes, F.T.R.I."—Dr. Hayes himself, obviously.

Inside the cover, printed on the end papers of the book, was a map of northern Canada and the complex of islands above. A *complete* map—and despite his incredulity More knew, somehow, that the outlines were accurate. Along Lancaster Sound a broken line ran to meet a solid line; it was scarcely a surprise, by now, to find one labelled "Track of H.M.S. *Resolute*, August — September, 1850" and the other "Track of sledge expedition under Lieut. J. McLintock, 1850-51." The two met at Griffith's Island, in a large shaded rectangle marked "Disputed area of tracks — see Frontispiece."

The Frontispiece map showed the area in detail. Across it ran tracks marked "Route of the returning sledge parties, according to Lieut. McLintock"; "Routes of search parties under Capt, Austin, Lieut. More, Lieut. Barnes"; and "Actual route of the sledge parties, as suggested by Capt. Austin." All these, More realised with a new and dream-like acceptance, were next year's events. Numbly, he turned back to the log entries and on to the end of the chapter.

"Throughout the last fifty miles, from where he first found open water, McLintock was expecting the ships to meet him. The party pressed on, across the melted pools and treacherous hummocks; skirting the dangerous edges of the pack; wet through and exhausted, dragging their sick and injured colleagues. In due course they struck across to the islands, and rounded the cape from which they last saw the winter anchorage. The ships were not there; and at that moment, effectively, began one of the most famous trials in naval history."

The next chapter was entitled "What Really Happened?" With a kind of desperation, More read on.

"Austin's 'bare acquittal' and the return of his sword could not satisfy the English public. In their opinion, the crew's testimony supporting Austin was mere evidence of conspiracy. The great explorer had basely deserted his professional rival, abandoning many of his own sailors to..." Behind him, More heard the cabin door open and close.

Diana Hayes stood there, shedding her gloves and opening her jacket as he had done before. She barely glanced at the open book in his hands. Now, her expression said plainly, the need for pretence was past. She moved towards him with assurance, her gaze so compelling that any resistance he might offer sank without trace. He knew, intellectually, that he should brandish the book and demand an explanation, but this short, dark-haired girl had him in thrall.

She came up to tiptoes, hung one arm about his neck and fastened her lips to his. Overwhelmed, More crushed her to him, appalled by the strength of the desire he had been suppressing for so long. He had to put an immediate stop to this, present the incredible evidence of the book to Captain Austin, but he couldn't find strength to act. Her hand came down past his waist, down to take him where he lived as she took a half-step to the side, hooking one leg around his. "Stop it...let go," he whispered, but failed to disengage her hand. His knuckles brushed her bare leg where somehow the seam of her skirt had parted, and helplessly he took hold, battening his lips over hers again...

"Mr. More!"

Slowly and with infinite reluctance More released her, turning to the men in the doorway. If the Captain's interruption had been two minutes later it would have been much harder to regain any kind of decorum. Behind her father, where the Captain couldn't see her, Evelyn Hayes had momentarily shed her cover: her expression was pure glee, without malice, at Diana's frustration.

"One law for the men and another for the officers, Mr. More?"

More swallowed hard and reached for the book. He had let it fall to the table –

Gone. The only time Diana could possibly have snatched it was just a second ago, as More faced Hayes and the Captain. It must now be in one of her hands, both thrust deep into the pockets of her jacket. Her expression was as clear as "England expects...": if he spoke, it would be a double betrayal. Hell would have no fury like *this* woman scorned, he suspected; her anger might put a rope around his neck.

Dr. Hayes's expression was grim, but otherwise unreadable. How far will he go to preserve his secret, thought More—will he see me discredited, or even hanged? Had he and Diana arranged this, seeing him enter the cabin? Determination came to him—he would *not* be used. It was his duty to speak.

At that precise moment there was an extraordinary sensation underfoot, as if the outside pressure had suddenly forced the ship up out of the pack. A cry of amazement rang out on deck, and— utterly impossible—a beam of sunlight stabbed down through the open hatch, framing Evelyn's head in brilliant gold against the gloom of the passage.

There was a rush of footsteps overhead, and Brown appeared silhouetted in the hatchway. "Captain, sir! Captain Austin!" Fear and incredulity rang in his voice.

"Here I am, Brown. Gangway, there!" Austin led the rush to the deck. More brought up the rear, ushering Diana ahead. Like the others he emerged blinking, first at the sunlight, then with disbelief. Minutes before the *Resolute* had been fast in the Arctic ice, buried in the gloom of winter—now she sat in the middle of a city square, her black hull sunk into its smooth surface. Sunlit buildings towered around her.

For the rest of his life, More remembered and profited by the Captain's example at that moment. Faced with the unexpected, it is better to give an order, any order, than to allow fear and surprise to paralyse one's command; but Austin swept the scene once with his eyes and gave the one order involving *all* the crew, and entirely appropriate:

"Clear for action! Pipe to quarters!"

For every man aboard, reflexes and training took over. The *Resolute* wasn't a man-o'-war and there wasn't a great deal to be done, but it galvanised everyone into action despite the spectacle over the side. The pipes shrilled along the ship, bosun's mates bawled "All hands on deck!" and the crew came tumbling up out of the hatches, pulling on the cold-weather gear they no longer needed. "Issue small arms!" the Captain ordered, and pistols and cutlasses appeared like magic. The marines came clattering up, muskets at the ready, to fall in by the mainmast.

"Guns cleared for action, sir," the breathless gunner's mate reported.

"Load, and run out," Austin snapped. In another minute, the *Resolute*'s teeth were fully shown.

A short pause ensued, time to take in details of their new surroundings. The city square around them was set with flower beds and statues. Some of the buildings around it seemed modern, but their stone was weathered and overlaid with smoke deposits. Others defied belief: the tallest in view, towering over closer buildings, seemed to be faced entirely with metal and glass. The *Resolute*'s prow pointed directly to a low structure, mainly wood and glass, on the edge of the square. A sign along its roof said

"Information Centre".

Dr. Hayes pointed it out. "I'd say, sir, from the spelling of 'Center', that we're in your country somewhere."

Austin gave him a look that spoke volumes. "God forbid," was his only comment, as he turned to survey the square.

There weren't many people about, but the passers-by were reacting to the *Resolute's* appearance in their city. People were streaming towards the ship from all directions, most of them young. There were girls, More realised, dressed like Diana in her sailor's costume, others in astonishingly short skirts, and men in styles he just couldn't believe. It's an illusion, or a nightmare, he thought.

"Hey man," one apparition shouted, "can we come aboard?"

"Stand by to repel boarders," snapped the Captain. The marines moved smartly to the rails.

"We want to come aboard!" The youngsters were shouting and clapping, pressing around the ship, and the crowd was swiftly growing. Some of the seamen were wavering. "Stand fast, all hands!" bellowed Austin.

On the starboard side, a youth was boosted up by his friends to catch the ship's rail. A quartermaster aimed a blow at him with a belaying pin and the fellow plunged back into the crowd. At almost the same moment a cutlass flashed in the bows as an A.B. slashed at someone clinging to the bowsprit. Waves of anger spread through the crowd, good humour evaporating like the frost off the shrouds.

"A musket volley over their heads," Austin called to the sergeant of marines. The guns banged raggedly, producing not the expected rout, but a fresh wave of laughter followed by cheering.

"They think we're some kind of entertainment, sir!" More exclaimed, his sanity under strain.

"We'll disabuse 'em of the notion, Mr. More. Gunner's Mate—a ball at that statue over there!"

Without the usual noises of wind and sea the cannon's crack

was deafening, echoing back from the surrounding buildings. With the ship firmly fixed, at that range the ball couldn't possibly miss. The ball split the statue and rebounded towards the "Information Centre", from which came a great crash of breaking glass. The crowd scattered, screaming; several of them had been injured by splinters flying from the statue. In less than a minute the square was empty. Several figures could still be seen fleeing down the side streets.

"That's better," said the Captain. "Stand by, all hands."

"Shall we remove jackets and furs, sir?" More asked. They seemed to be in a hot summer's morning, and even with his own jacket open More was sweating freely.

"I think not, Mr. More. All this may be some deadly hallucination, like the flying machines we saw before. If we expose ourselves to the Arctic night, thinking it's magically become the English summer, maybe we'll join Franklin on the list of missing ships. Meantime, Mr. More, you'll take a party below and check for damage. If these events are real and we suddenly return to the Arctic, I don't want to learn at that moment that our timbers are smashed below the waterline." Looking over the side they could see that, despite the impression that the ship had been lifted, the paving of the square was no further below the white riband than the ice had been before.

The ship was intact all the way to her keel, as far as he could determine. It was strange to be below with no sound of water coming through the hull, not even the cranks and groans of the ice. Stranger still the new noises, which could only be subterranean happenings in the city itself. Every few minutes there came a deep, eerie rumbling, as if some great machine was passing near them through the earth.

Going through the 'tweendecks, strangely deserted and quiet as if the ship was in drydock, he saw Diana Hayes coming to meet him. She was projecting the same irresistible attraction as before, though a new and grimmer determination had been added. He moved towards her and was halted as she caught him at the waist, possessively, but keeping him at arm's length.

"Now listen, sailor boy." And listen he did, mesmerised, despite the difference in their heights. "I wouldn't have come on to you like that if I hadn't wanted to. I was glad of the chance to do something I'd wanted to do since I came aboard. If I had the chance I would go all the way with you, without shame and without guilt—not like the girls of your time. But that is the point: I'm not from your time. I'm from the late 20th century, your future—you could be my great-grandfather, though I don't think so...and I shall have to go back there. It's not so much because of my work, though that means a lot to me, but simply that I can't stay here. The aliens are disturbing time enough as it is—my 'father' will tell you—" More noticed the way she said 'father' and was suddenly jealous. "Now something much more serious has happened. It may even be our fault, and that's what I have to find out. It may even mean that we *can't* return to the future, and if not, then you're mine, Lieutenant." Her hands clenched without warning, making him catch his breath. "Now we both have our duty to do—go to it!"

She turned and left him, not looking back. God, what a handful she would be, literally and figuratively. What kind of world could it be, where a respectable young woman—assuming that she *was* respectable—could act like that?

A world with books describing events still to happen; where men dressed like scarecrows and women like harlots; a world of glass and metal buildings..."I'm from the late 20th century," she had said, while he stood nodding like a fool. *Is that where we are now?*

He arrived on deck not comprehending that wild thought, but convinced of the urgency of sharing it with the Captain. He found Austin in no mood to receive wild thoughts—Dr. Hayes had already assailed him with too many.

"...alternate worlds, Doctor, alternate poppycock. I ask you to account for a crisis which has overtaken the ship and you give me metaphysical drivel about how a cat can be alive and not alive at the same time. I'm not a man to trifle with, Dr. Hayes: there's only one cat of consequence aboard this ship, and that one's not in a box, it's in a bag—from which it has been out once already on this voyage, in an incident concerning you. You know more than you're saying, sir, and I mean to have it from you. Who are those Plymouth men, and why are they not at their posts now?"

Hayes began to reply, though, from the helpless spreading of his hands, it would not have been an answer to please Austin. In the quiet, however, the cry of the lookout drowned him out.

"Unknown vessel on the port bow!"

It wasn't exactly a *vessel*, though More would have been equally stumped for the right word. It was some kind of enclosed carriage, painted black and white, and apparently self-propelled: there were no horses, and the throb of an engine could plainly be heard. Two uniformed men emerged from it, one carrying a curious form of speaking-trumpet.

"British police uniforms," said Hayes. "Taken with the other clues around us, Captain, I would say the year here is somewhere in the nineteen-eighties. We have swung to within twenty years of my own time."

"Welcome home," said Austin, dismissing the absurdity. "Ahoy there! Stand where you are, that's close enough."

The amplified reply boomed eerily around the square, but its tinny overtones couldn't mask the challenge to the Captain's authority. "This is Inspector Scott of the City Police. I don't know what kind of stunt this is, and since we already have several people injured and considerable damage to property, I don't care. Lay down your weapons immediately and come out here on to the Square!"

Austin wouldn't entertain that. "This is Her Majesty's Ship *Resolute*, in the Arctic out of England in the year 1850..." He had compromised to the extent of throwing back his fur hood, but had refused to follow Dr. Hayes and Evelyn in shedding furs altogether. "I don't know how we came here, if indeed we truly *are* here, or how soon we may return. Until I have more information, no man will enter or leave this ship!"

"Look, I don't intend to stand here and argue," shouted the Inspector. "The Special Branch are already in position, the Anti-Terrorist squad is on the way and military assistance is on standby. Turn those cannon inboard, lay down your other weapons and surrender to my men, or the consequences will be serious!"

"*Late* 1980s," murmured Evelyn. Hayes nodded. Austin made no reply to them or to the threat, and after a moment the Inspector turned on his heel. He and his companion returned to their conveyance and mechanical voices could be heard from it as it moved away. Another appeared almost at once from a side street, this one plain black and armoured; it bumped up on to the square and smoke began to issue from it as it moved upwind of the ship.

Dr. Hayes laid a firm hand on Austin's arm. "Discourage that, Captain," he said urgently. Evidently he thought it no time for niceties and however reluctantly, Austin took his word. "Come to bear and fire!" he roared. The bow and stern guns swivelled and spoke together; the black side of the vehicle caved in and it swerved drunkenly away from the ship, disappearing from view behind the wrecked 'Information Centre'.

"Just in time," said Hayes. "We're hardly in a position to withstand a gas attack." Nobody knew what he meant and Austin didn't pause to ask. "They won't take that lying down, Mr. More. Take cover from sharpshooters, there—Mister Mate, get screens up along the side of the ship!"

Austin drew Barnes aside; as they pointed out at the Sun and drew diagrams in the air, More guessed they were discussing the ship's position. Scanning around, he noticed with concern black-clad figures moving from cover to cover on the surrounding roofs. Glimpsing one through the telescope, he saw that the man was armed and hooded, and began assessing how much protection the remaining deck cargo would afford.

"I've been here before," said Evelyn Hayes, behind him. "It looked differently, but this is Glasgow, Scotland, I believe." More was about to order her below, but he noticed that she pronounced

'Glasgow' correctly, unlike so many Americans, and paused in case she had valuable information. "If you turn your glass on that statue there, Lieutenant, I think you'll find it's Queen Victoria."

More looked, and began to explode in indignation before partial comprehension and shock took over. "Queen Victoria— that old...? ...*old*...."

He turned to face her, and she nodded. "You're getting it, Lieutenant. Better convince the Captain that it's true."

"And then what?" asked More. A helpless look crossed Evelyn's face, but before she could answer a strange grinding noise began, overlaid by the sound of an engine much louder than the Police carriages'. The noise grew in volume, echoing in the silent square, and into view came a vehicle olive-green in colour, and as heavily armoured as *Resolute* herself was against the ice. It was propelled, apparently, by metal belts underneath it, doing considerable damage to the roadway—but by far the worst thing about it was the extraordinary cannon mounted on top, swinging with nightmare ease to bear on the ship.

"That's what's known as a tank, Captain," Hayes confided, keeping his voice down. "Your cannon will make little impression on that steel armour, I'm afraid. And their own shells are packed with explosives—just a few of them will tear this wooden ship apart."

Austin studied it, past the shields they had put up. "Where's the entrance to it—is that a hatch in the roof?"

A man wearing a metal helmet had put his head through the opening. An inhuman voice, mechanical and deafening, rang across the square.

"The City Centre has been placed under martial law. Whatever the explanation, your guns are to be turned over to the Army without delay. In your own terms, you must strike your ensign. You have five minutes to surrender: otherwise we shall disable your cannon with our own fire."

The Captain looked even more grim. "We'll have to risk leaving the ship," he said at last. "Mr. More, take five men and capture that machine. If you can't get at the men inside it, should they close the hatch, be sure you spike that gun before you return here. We'll try to give you cover against their snipers—"

Hayes was going to raise some objection, but there was no need for it. The city faded as if it were mirage after all, with a sensation as if the ship had come off the top of a great wave. A moment later the deck tilted: this time the ship really was sliding off a wave-crest. The *Resolute* was back in open water—and back in the Arctic, to judge by the sudden cold in the wind.

Again the Captain was first to react. "*Make sail!* Get some way on her, bring her round to catch the wind. Man the lead, and get someone with keen eyes to the main-top—" His eye lit on the third lieutenant, as furious activity broke out. "Your sextant, Mr. Barnes, where the devil are we?" Must I tell everyone his job, his tone said plainly. Barnes vanished for the instrument.

More helped Evelyn into her jacket, then shrugged into his own. The sun was still in the sky, though appreciably nearer the horizon. They were in Barrow Strait again, he guessed, but obviously not in winter. Barnes was going to find his calculations difficult, with his chronometer time meaningless and no date to look up in the *Nautical Almanac*.

"We are at sea now, Dr. Hayes, and it appears to be summer. Those are kitty-wake and ivory-gulls over the water, are they not?" Austin's tone suggested that a simple answer even to that might be too much to hope for. "Is the ship safe for the moment, do you suppose?"

"Yes, sir, I suppose so—for the moment."

"Which is just one among an infinity of possible moments, you'd have me believe—whatever it may mean. We'll get to the bottom of what's happened now, if you don't mind—in my cabin, out of this wind. You may as well come too, Miss Hayes: of the three of you, you seem to be the only one with a sensible head on your shoulders."

Evelyn gave him a look that seemed strangely out of character, as if she resented the compliment, but she allowed the Captain to usher her below. More followed, though not ordered to do so. Though he couldn't see the full picture, he knew that he had several of the vital details. Austin, however, was very much in charge as they seated themselves around his table.

"You've tried to explain yourself in your own way, Dr. Hayes, and you've made a hash of it. For the moment you'll oblige me by just answering the questions I put to you, in plain English if you please. To begin with, sir, who are you? and perhaps more importantly, *what* are you? You're like no man of science that ever I met."

"I'm not one, in the ordinary sense," said Hayes. "I am in fact a historian, though with the means of study we have at our disposal, history is more a science, rather than an art." Austin's eye met More's and a sceptical look passed between them; it would not have occurred to either of them that history was not a science. But the point was too minor to challenge.

"My speciality is the history of your time, and I study it from the viewpoint of the late twentieth century," Hayes went on. "That is my time, through which I have grown and aged in the normal way, having been born a hundred years from what you call 'now'. I was born on the hundredth anniversary of your departure from England, Captain; I think that's why your story always fascinated me...and in the year 1998, my colleagues and I left our own time to find out for ourselves what happened to you."

"Colleagues," Austin said flatly. More guessed that he was trying to imagine Hayes as a professional associate of the troublemakers in the fo'c'sle. Hayes missed the point entirely.

"Neither of them is my daughter, Captain, as you may have guessed. The rôle of women is changing even in your own time. There is a woman now in Egypt, by the name of Florence Nightingale—I could tell you what she's going to do, but there's no point because you can't verify it. Worse still, some destructive impulse might make you try to prevent it, and I suspect that in some versions of history you would succeed."

"Stick to facts, please, Doctor, not what even you admit to be conjectures. Verification is just the point, is it not. Can anything you have said so far be verified, by any test I might accept?"

"I doubt it, Captain," Hayes said wearily. "All our aim was to prevent you realising the truth about us. I could tell you things which are happening now, on the other side of the world, but you have no way to check up on them. We brought virtually nothing with us from our own time to betray what we are—though Diana had a theory, which she insisted on putting to the test, that any devices or manners which seemed strange to you would be laughed off as curiosities, or eccentricity."

The book was not evidence, More realised: it could be part of some very elaborate hoax. That Hayes didn't mention it showed its importance—and he didn't know More had seen it! I have a trump card to play, thought More, if he tries to misdirect us—we may have to summon Diana and demand that she produce it. Come to that, where was Diana? He hadn't seen her since the beginning of the bizarre events in the city—*events which weren't mentioned in the book...*

If Austin noticed More stiffen, he didn't think it significant. "'Curious' or 'eccentric' are not the words I'd use of those Plymouth men, Doctor. Latterly their behaviour was far more strange than yours, and they failed to appear at all when we piped to quarters. Yet you speak of your expedition from the future as if they had no part of it. Who are they, and what's their interest in you?"

"I don't know," said Hayes. But in response to Austin's scowl, he went on, reluctantly: "I believe—and it's only a belief—that they are not of this world."

"Don't let the crew hear a word of that," said Austin, with all his authority behind the words. "What are you saying, man—that we have entertained angels unawares?"

"Not angels, Captain. Aliens. Intelligent beings from another world, or androids—creatures made by true aliens, to masquerade as humans. But creatures from some other world in space, not from some fanciful world of the supernatural."

"Fanciful worlds," mused Austin. "You come from the future, but can't prove it. They come from space, and have apparently vanished into it. We have been plucked from the ice into a locality strange enough to defy all reason, which you casually tell me is the Scotland of another time—and now we are in open water, in what is very obviously Arctic summer. You claim to know what is happening elsewhere in the world, but there's no point in telling me. But by God you'll answer me one such question, because lives are at stake and it's vital to the success of the expedition. *Have I missed the rendezvous with McLintock?*"

"You missed it last time," said Hayes.

Total silence fell in the cramped cabin. Evelyn put a restraining hand on Hayes's arm; he turned to face her. "The events we've all been through aren't in the log," he said. "This is another alternate."

"We're back into your conjectures, Doctor," Austin pointed out. "This was where you and I parted company last time, and I expect a better explanation now. On the face of it, the expression 'alternate worlds' is meaningless." He slapped his hands alternately on the table. "This world, then *that* world...this world, then that. You make no sense."

Hayes chuckled, though the relentless inquisition clearly had him under strain. "It's a trick of language—usages change in a hundred years. Not alternate, then—alternative. This world *and* that, both going on in parallel."

"We're back to that damned cat in the box," said Austin, his tone threatening. "You're on dangerous ground, sir. Don't try me too far."

Evelyn restrained Hayes again. "Let me tell it, then. The story of Schrödinger's Cat is an illustration of some extraordinary discoveries we have made about the nature of reality. You don't know what radioactive decay is, so you must take my word that it's a process which occurs randomly, but at an overall rate governed by time. If you put a cat into a box with a phial of poison, to be released by the radioactive process, then after a certain interval of time the chances that the cat was alive or dead would be exactly equal." She looked from Austin to More and back, gauging their reactions. "You can't tell without opening the box. In a sense, the cat is both dead and alive. When you open the box, if the cat is alive our world goes on from there—but there is another world which you cannot perceive, in which the cat is dead."

"Nonsense," said Austin, sitting back. "It's only good manners, Miss Hayes, that keeps me from using a stronger word. I cannot understand why you present this to me as if it was important. I have listened to it twice, and my patience is wearing very thin." He sat suddenly forward and stabbed a finger at Hayes across the table. "You have one chance, Doctor, and you'll make a fool of me at your peril. What the devil has this rambling about a cat to do with McLintock?"

"You missed the rendezvous," Hayes said despairingly. "You and your crew swore that you were there; McLintock and his party swore that they were there; but no meeting took place. It was one of the most famous trials of the century and is still one of the great mysteries of the sea. You suggested McLintock's navigation was faulty; historians wrangle over whether you were right. But if you were both right, and yet you missed each other, it could only be because somebody interfered. It's as if you opened the box and found the phial broken but the cat unharmed: either somebody replaced the poison or somebody gave the cat an antidote."

'The 'aliens'?" said More. "Diana said they were 'disturbing time enough as it is'?"

Hayes relaxed slightly. "A paradoxical turn of phrase, when you think about it...But yes, the aliens might be to blame, as I thought. You saw their flying machines, you saw a spacecraft enter the atmosphere—all the indications of a large expedition arriving, and then nothing, not even a departure. My theory is that they took over the Earth on which you made the rendezvous, leaving humanity otherwise undisturbed on the alternate one, created by their meddling, on which you missed it. They used the ship as a historical pivot—moved it in time, perhaps, from one Arctic winter to another without you realising, and then put you back in 1851 after the rendezvous had been missed."

"But something much more spectacular has happened to us," Austin pointed out. "Are you suggesting that a third 'alternate' has been generated? It must be, because we realised we had been moved...and we have returned far out of place. We could be anywhere—the other end of the Passage, even—and what year is it now, I'd like to know? This is outrageous, Dr. Hayes. It's plainly the result of your meddling—the so-called 'aliens' appear relatively innocent!"

"We don't know how they behave on the alternate Earth," said Hayes. "Do they share it with humanity, do they rule, or do they destroy us? The evidence suggests several interventions in history—they may have taken Earth away from us several times." Having gained an advantage with that sobering thought, he pressed on. "Besides, I don't think we're responsible for the new track; at least, not directly. There's a cat in a box that we have still to open."

Austin sighed. "With reluctance, sir, I ask you—what do you mean by that?"

"At the moment when we returned to the Arctic, Captain, you were sending Lieutenant More off the ship to attack the tank. Until you took that decision, the unresolved question was whether people would be allowed on or off the ship, perhaps thereby 'anchoring' it in the future. When you took that decision, you were in effect about to open Shrödinger's box—and the result, as it seems, was to displace us from the future and return us to the Arctic."

Hayes paused, but Austin was baffled. More saw the point, however, more clearly than Hayes himself anticipated. "And with your talk of swings and pivots, Doctor, the implication is that the starting point of the swing might also have involved me."

"We had just found you in what you would term a compromising situation—"

"More compromising to you, sir, if the truth be told. The unresolved question of that moment, on which I had in fact then taken my decision, was whether or not to reveal the existence of your book 'Voyage to Controversy'."

Hayes was taken aback; Austin obviously about to demand explanation. More pressed on. "It's a book, sir, written by Dr. Hayes in his future persona, which describes our voyage in detail—down to the very fireball which Brown and I saw only minutes before the crisis—and goes on to relate how we missed the rendezvous with Lieutenant McLintock, how you were court-martialled, and I don't know what else. What Dr. Hayes would describe as 'trying to open the box' was, presumably, my decision to tell you about the book, despite Miss Hayes's...counter-persuasion."

"Then I'll see it now," Austin replied firmly. "Dr. Hayes, I have a scientific background, as any serious explorer must have, but if there's anything at all to substantiate your fantastic story then I have a right to see it. As things stand, there's only one element in my experience which strikes a chord with it, and that's the feeling every seaman knows in mid-ocean—especially in the Arctic— that he and his shipmates are in a different world, occupied by themselves alone."

"It's called 'breakoff phenomenon'" said Evelyn Hayes. "Pilots experience it at great altitudes, and space travellers, too—human ones, I mean—far out on journeys to the Moon."

"Fascinating," said Austin. "I've often regretted the fact—and said as much to my officers—that the great age of exploration seemed to be ending, with only the Poles still to reach. And now you lay all of this before me...but first I must insist that you lay this remarkable book before me. Now, if you please."

"Who has it?" asked More. Dr. Hayes and Evelyn looked blank. "Miss Diana had it from me. Where is she now?"

"I've seen wondering that," said Evelyn. "I haven't seen her since we materialised in the city."

"Neither have I," said Hayes, alarmed. "She couldn't have left the ship...?"

"I don't think so," More interrupted. "I met her below decks, going for'ard. She said she had her duty to do; some research for you, I assumed."

"She went to check on the aliens, the idiot!" cried Hayes. "She said nothing to anyone about it...Captain, they must still be somewhere aboard."

"There's been no time to search," Austin agreed, "but we'll have it done now, if Brown doesn't already have it in hand. Come with me, Mr. More."

"I can hear that helicopter again," said Evelyn Hayes.

Everyone froze—More and Austin because they didn't know what she meant. But in a moment they too heard the distinctive beat of the flying machine which had passed the *Resolute* in the fog, weeks before. Another moment brought the sound of a scuffle on the planking overhead, and the sound of a body falling to the deck. The motion of the ship changed sharply as the wheel was thrown over.

This time More was first up out of the hatch. As he reached the deck the ship came up into the eye of the wind and hung there in irons, the banging of the sails drowning out the noise of the approaching aircraft. On the poop the Plymouth seamen were again gathered in their strange inward-facing circle, including the man who now had the wheel. The helmsman lay unconscious at his feet. And within the circle Diana Hayes stood motionless, as if mesmerised, staring towards the man who now controlled the ship. None of them wore furs, despite the wind.

More's reaction was virtually instinctive. The aliens, or androids, or whatever they were, had waited until the crew stood down from action stations before making their move. The sailors on deck were unarmed, the marines were once again below. But More still had his pistol, whose drawing he could not afterwards recall; he raised it, sighted and fired, with a clear shot at the usurper of the wheel. The man released the spokes and fell back a step, and as the circle was broken Diana came out of her trance.

As More had to admit afterwards, he had no idea how she would react; but he would have made a wager that neither a scream nor a faint would be on the agenda. What did happen was that she lunged after the wounded man, and, bringing her hands over her head in a blow that looked curiously oriental, smashed her captor of a moment before in the solar plexus. The backward step became a career and the seaman vanished head-first over the taffrail. To More's astonishment the other men of the clique at once ran aft in two lines, passing to either side of Diana and the wheel to dive like porpoises over the rail.

The 'helicopter' at once veered towards them, coming into plain sight from behind the sails. Apart from the rotating airfoils it resembled a great whirring insect, with a golden body and windows like high-placed bulbous eyes. As it dropped astern of the *Resolute* the downwash from its blades swept over them; the sails filled with a final crack and the ship fell off on to the port tack, heeling over as the true wind gained control and forced her around. A seaman—a true one—rushed aft to catch the wheel at the null point in its deadly spin.

"Man overboard!" roared Austin. "Stand by to come about—"

"Don't do that, Captain!" Hayes seized Austin's arm once more. "Keep going—put on more sail, if you can!"

"Monstrous, Doctor! No man can live for more than minutes in arctic water—"

"Whatever else they are, they're not men. We still don't know whether they're aliens or living machines, but my money's on the latter. But what we *do* know is far too much—we must escape or they'll destroy us. There's a squall coming and it'll give us cover to dodge; we must hope that when the machine is fully loaded it won't have enough fuel to search for us. But above all, Captain, now that we know what we know, *we must get away*."

It was very nearly one challenge too many, but after a moment Austin gave way. He snapped the necessary orders to Brown, whose bellows brought the crew back on deck, back to action stations, and turned the ship towards the cover of the approaching squall. The flying machine, picking up the swimmers far astern, was already being hidden by the onrushing mist.

"Now that we know what we know?" Austin repeated, as the sun disappeared and the wind rose. "We know perilous little, Doctor, or so it seemed only minutes ago."

"We already knew that we were on a new time-track," said Hayes. "But now we know something much more important: we are on the one occupied by the aliens. They do not have a time-track in which you made the rendezvous with McLintock; that version of history may have been wiped out altogether. But in this world, we are here—and they are here—and we all know about one another. Unless their plans for mankind are wholly beneficial, the whole ship and the five of us here in particular are a great threat to them. We must alert your government, and mine, and all the rest.."

"And it falls to me to do this, while I face court-martial for deserting McLintock," Austin added. "I consider myself entitled to your full support, Dr. Hayes, when we return to England—and it will be England first, let me assure you."

"You shall have it, sir," Hayes promised. "But things in England may not be as you suppose. We are in the Arctic, and perhaps in 1851, but not the 1851 of my past—not the 1851 of my book. Many other things may be different. The whole world is unknown, Captain; we can count on nothing that we used to know."

"Our time machine may not be there," said Diana to More. "Even if it is, it will be a long time if ever before we get back to it. The Captain gets back the world of mystery that he longed for, but we may all of us get what we most want."

She seized his arm and squeezed it, much to More's embarrassment; but the Captain didn't notice the breach of decorum on his quarter-deck. He was gazing out over the cold sea, his mind ranging the infinite vistas of exploration beyond.

Notes

In origin, this story goes back to 6th May, 1968, in the Golden Eagle Hotel in Prestwick, Ayrshire. Charles Muir and I were running the Prestwick Folk Song Club, and that night we had booked Martin Carthy and Dave Swarbrick. It was a great success, one of the best nights we ever put on. In the course of it Martin Carthy sang "Lord Franklin", with a humorous introduction which—I afterwards found out—was all made up. "...the search included the U.S. Navy, which consisted of about two rowing-boats at the time; and incidentally, it was the U.S. Navy, in their two rowing-boats, which found the North-West Passage, while searching for Lord Franklin... Sir John Franklin, I beg his pardon... the world's most unsuccessful explorer." Not a word of truth in any of it, except for the 'Sir John'.

I learned the true story from an article which crossed my desk when I working for the Fisheries Division of Christian Salvesen (Managers) Ltd in 1970. Whether it was because of the contrast with Martin's introduction or not I don't know, but in the summer of 1971, after I had become a full-time writer, I too "dreamed a dream... concerning Franklin, and his gallant crew." Unlike the narrator of the song, I didn't think it true, but I knew it was a winner—to the extent of resisting all attempts by my family to wake me. They had been seized by an unaccountable determination to wake me up, because it was such a beautiful day, although they knew I'd been working late. What was even odder was that I did get back to sleep, about three times, and each time resumed the dream where it left off. When I did get up I began at once to make notes, and the more I wrote down, the more I 'remembered'.

The quotes round 'remembered' are because the dream contained a great deal I didn't previously know, from Martin Carthy or the article. Some other influences were obvious—I had seen Alec Guinness in *HMS Defiant* only days before, for instance—but I had no previous knowledge that steam tenders were in use in Arctic exploration as early as 1850, to give just one example. When I realised that the 1850 expedition of HMS *Resolute* corresponded to my dream so closely, I decided to base the story on it.

The 1850-51 naval expedition was the subject of a parliamentary enquiry, because of allegations made by some of the civilian vessels searching for Franklin. There's a copy of the Proceedings, which included extensive extracts from the log, in a Special Collection at Glasgow University Library; and I was the first person ever to borrow it, in 120 years. I read quite a number of other books on polar exploration; A.L. Lloyd's book "Folk Song in England", and his LP 'First Person', provided the musical background.

I also discovered a reference to "Leaves from an Arctic Journal; or, 18 Months in the Polar Regions in Search of Sir John Franklin's Expedition in the Years 1850-51" by Lieutenant S. Osborn. The G.U. Library didn't have that, but the Strathclyde University Library did, and although G.U. graduates didn't have access to the Strathclyde Library at that time, I was able to read the book by courtesy of Barbara Dinning of the Library staff. I had the title wrong ("Stray Leaves...") but I've let it stand in the story: a little unfairly, because Lt. Osborn's book was very helpful on points of detail, but I've never been able to get over his remarks about his visit to the Faroe Islands. In their earlier indolence, it seems, the Faroese took from the sea only enough whales and seals to meet their immediate needs; but under missionary influence, they now slaughtered far more than they could possibly use—an example of Christian industry which Lt.

Osborn commended to us all for copying.

Apart from Austin, McLintock and Osborn, everyone I've placed aboard HMS *Resolute* is fictitious. Nor do I know of any real-life rivalry between Capt. Horatio Austin and Lieut. Leopold McLintock, the sledge travel expert who eventually found the tragic remains of Franklin's expedition; both men were dedicated to the search for Franklin, which was the main purpose of the voyage. There *was* a Dr. Hayes (different first name) with De Haven on the American ships Austin met past Lancaster Sound. He returned to the Arctic with Kane, on the expedition of 1852-54 on which the *Advance* was lost in the ice, and later commanded an expedition of his own, of which the *Encyclopedia Britannica* remarks, "his narrative is not to be depended upon."

In real life the four ships of Austin's flotilla wintered together in 1850-51, with Penny twenty miles away; they sent out eight search parties the following spring. After reaching Melville Island McLintock's party returned safely to the ships after 81 days despite their difficulties with the thawing ice. The ships returned to England in 1851, McLintock going with them again to the Arctic the following year. In 1853 Robert McLure, who had traversed the North-West passage from west to east by sledge, was picked up by the *Resolute* after his *Intrepid* was lost in the ice in 1851 at Mercy Bay, on Banks Island. (It was McLure who took on extra hands at Plymouth in 1850. His previous ship, HMS *Investigator*, was wrecked in 1848 and her remains were found on the seabed in July 2010.) By the end of the mystery in 1857, the search for Franklin had effectively resolved the geography of the North-West Passage and the surrounding region: perhaps one of the few explorations in history to receive so much impetus from humanitarian motives. A desk made of wood from the *Resolute* was afterwards presented to the White House, where it still remains in the Oval Office.

The first draft of 'In the Arctic, Out of Time' didn't get placed anywhere, due partly to the effects on the market of the 1971 British postal strike. In the 1980s, when I began to write fiction again, I put it back on the market and this time it was accepted by *Isaac Asimov's Science Fiction Magazine*, with a new ending requested by the editor Gardner Dozois making it clear which time-track the characters are on at the end. There was a two-year hiatus, and another two-year delay before publication, but when it appeared in 1989—18 years after I wrote it!—they gave it the cover, and it got nine recommendations for the Nebula Award.

'In the Arctic...' is alternative history from the outset, and that allowed me to take some liberties with Glasgow's George Square. It does have room for HMS *Resolute*, just (I paced it out), but the ship would be hard up against the monument to Sir Walter Scott and since that didn't suit me, I removed it. The 1960s "Information Centre" was long gone by the 1980s, and 'our' equestrian statue of Queen Victoria dates from 1854, shows her as a young woman, and faces the wrong way to be seen from the ship. Troops and tanks were brought into Glasgow during the postwar unrest in 1919, and stationed in the Cattlemarket on the Gallowgate after 'the battle of George Square' between protestors and the police. The prediction that it might happen again by the late 1980s didn't seem unreasonable in 1971, or even in the mid-1980s.

There were still other oddities, however. In 1988, I had wanted some historical background on Central America for a novel. I had a drink with Dr. Euan MacKie of the Hunterian Museum, who's an expert on the Maya. He was quite happy to direct me to the sources I needed, but was I happy to work with this kind of material? Oh yes, I said, I've done historical research for other fiction; and I told him about the parliamentary report.

The following week, Gardner Dozois asked me to change the names of the people on the ship back to the real ones. So I applied to borrow the report again: but someone else had taken it out. I rang Euan MacKie, and he wasn't the one who had it, so I had to request its recall; and when I got it, whoever had taken it out—just after I'd told Euan about it—was the only other borrower, ever, in what was now 136 years. I suspected it must be Euan checking up on me, but he denied all knowledge of the other borrower.

I'd forgotten why I'd changed the names, originally. The problem was that half the people on the ship had names like Armstrong, Aldrin or Langley: astronauts, NASA administrators,

NASA research centres! The ship's musician was called Organ; the sailmaker, who was also a singer, was called Record; and other plain seafaring lads had aristocratic French surnames, probably descended from refugees from the Terror. Nobody would have believed them in a work of fiction; there were only a couple of the historical names I could use.

There was one other change that Gardner insisted on. Twice in the action the ship encounters a helicopter (which didn't happen in 1850, though they did log "a rocket or shooting star" in the night). I chose a helicopter because for story purposes, whatever they met had to hover, fly slowly, make a distinctive noise, have a light underneath, create a downdraught and look utterly bizarre to 19th century sailors. But Gardner had decided he wanted to feature the second encounter on the magazine cover, and he was worried that a helicopter might make it look too much like a scene from the Tall Ships Race. It is a science fiction magazine, after all. So he made just two changes. Where Evelyn Hayes says, "I can hear that helicopter again", he substituted the word 'ship'; and where I described it as "like a huge, whirring insect", he substituted 'glowing'. Sure enough, that was enough for the artist Bob Walters to paint something like a giant ladybird.

The change was made after I checked and approved the proofs, and I wasn't very happy about that, but I was assured no other changes had been made. So the story was published, and then I got a letter from the late John Brunner. (If you knew John, you'll know that he was much into folk music as well as SF.) John's questions were both about the same scene in the story: first, did they really have an accordion, only a year or so after it was invented? I could answer that from the log extracts: yes, in fact one of the sledge parties took it with them. (The log doesn't record what the rest of the crew thought about that.) The other thing was, Diana overhears the singing of *Saint James's Hospital*. "There's an American version," she says, so giving away that she's from the future, relative to 1850, because *Saint James's Hospital* goes back to 1790, and *Saint James' Infirmary* only to 1905. A.L. Lloyd was my source for that; but now, here was John saying I'd got it wrong. I checked my copy of the proofs—quite correct. But after I'd returned the other one, some eagle-eyed and helpful copy-editor had changed the 'error' for me, so making nonsense of the whole paragraph.

Interestingly enough, there is also an American version of *Farewell Nancy*, sung for me by Meg Davis soon after the story came out. I can't help feeling that the 'In the Arctic...' saga still has a long way to go.

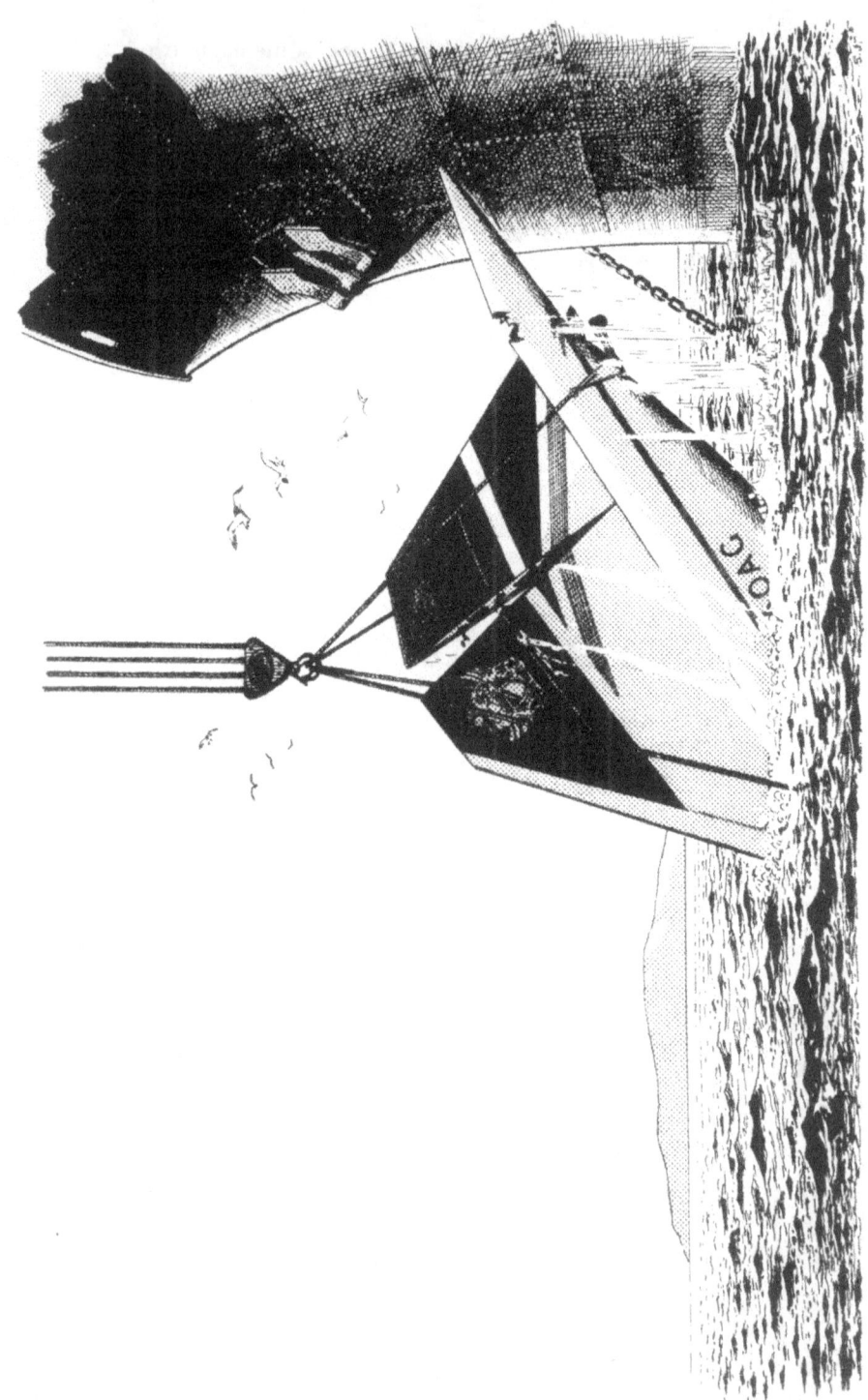

With Time Comes Concord

Pendleton had picked a poor time of day for his visit to Farnborough. In spring, summer and autumn the roads round the airfield were beautiful, thickly wooded, a pastoral setting in which the red-and-white Ministry of Defence direction signs would always seem incongruous. On this grey March day in 1969, after 5 p.m. and darkening early in the rain, the signs seemed more appropriate among the leafless trees: although some of the newer Ministry of Transport ones, like 'Tank Crossing', with its appropriate symbol inside the new-format European red triangle, still seemed wildly bizarre.

The hangars allocated to the Accident Section were on the south side of the airfield, near where the aviation pioneer S.F. Cody had built his string-and-bamboo plane. They needed some romantic connection on a day like this: as he followed the perimeter track the runways were swept by sheets of rain, away from the protection of the trees. A far cry from the glamour of the summer Air Shows, with Raymond Baxter's enthusiastic commentary broadcast to the nation.

Nevertheless, here he was: John Pendleton, ex-Flight Lieutenant (RAF), ex-Air Traffic Controller (Ministry of Civil Aviation, Prestwick) and now in the job he had been wangling for—Inspector of Accidents (Operations), in training, Accident Investigation Branch, Board of Trade; reporting to the Royal Aircraft Establishment for his first assignment.

Hangar T-49 was the largest, able to house several aircraft

reconstructions at once, lit by seemingly endless rows of overhead lights. Hot-air blowers struggled to beat the cold and damp outside. Spread over the floor, in great piles, were tons of metal wreckage—much of it unrecognisable, but parts all too obviously from a civil Viscount. The tail assembly, almost intact and propped up on a wooden frame in the distance, bore the British Midland logo; the crash had been on takeoff during a training flight from Manchester, just days before. A detailed plan of the airliner had been chalked on the floor, like the outline of a murder victim— though this was not where the 'deceased' had fallen. Among the wreckage two men squatted, in civvies like himself. Occasionally one of them would pick up a piece of metal, examine it, shake his head and put it back. A third, looking on, beckoned him over.

"John Pendleton, reporting."

"Bill Carstairs; I'm the Inspector (Engineering) on the current 'go-team'. This one has nothing to do with you," Carstairs went on, indicating the wreckage around them. "I was just looking over these chaps' shoulders till you got here—we'll leave them to get on with it. You know what the situation is? New fellas start off on light aircraft, and work up from there?"

"That's how it was explained to me," said Pendleton.

"Right. Well, it looks as if we have one in the Hebrides—you'll have been briefed on that? Three bodies have been found on the western shore of South Uist, and the doctor in Lochboisdale thinks they died from a plane crash. He's reported it to the local police, and it's gone up the chain until it reached the gate at which the big boss in London was notified. Now it's an AIB matter, and it needs you, me, and a qualified flight surgeon, which the RAF will supply. The Commander Flying here has fixed us seats on a Hercules to Benbecula at nineteen hundred hours. I take it you're all packed and ready to go?"

"Yes—except for parking my car. I'm only in a temporary space."

"Hand in your keys at the office, they'll take care of that for you. Listen, I know you're being thrown in at the deep end, but it's a baptism of fire for you. For as long as you remain with this Branch, when you're on the Readiness Roster, you can be sent anywhere in the world that you're needed, and the rest of us move up. In theory we can all be sent to Kuala Lumpur or worse, tomorrow, if we have to be. Is there anyone you have to notify—wife? girlfriend? family?"

"No, there isn't anyone. Not at the moment."

"Fine. But this is something to remember for the future: wife, family, kids, you can't make any commitments to them that are binding except when you're on annual leave. Maybe not even then, if we have a really bad one. That's what you've signed up for, and it's as well to know that right at the start."

Carstairs was voluble, even garrulous, Pendleton realised as they prepared for the flight. It could become irritating, but for the moment, when he had so much to learn, it was invaluable.

"...since the Chief briefed you first, you're in charge of the investigation. That gives you very considerable powers. You've been appointed to the Inspectorate by the Secretary of State, remember; once the Chief has decided there is to be an investigation, and he puts you in charge, even he can't take you off it. His decision can't be reversed, and you're protected by law from any kind of political pressure. There's not another country on Earth that gives its Inspectorate such autonomy."

"The only reason I was first was that I was in his office at the time!" Pendleton protested. "Essentially, he put down the phone and said, 'Would you like to start today?'"

"Well, make the most of it. The one thing you will have to watch, since there are fatalities involved, is that there can be conflicts with local coroners. An inquest is only supposed to determine the cause of death, but some coroners take that to include the cause of the accident, and try to apportion blame. Where it can get tricky is that they have powers to impound evidence, which would affect our work, of course, so you have to try to ensure that kind of conflict doesn't arise...There are a lot of pitfalls to watch for."

The conversation swiftly grew more technical. "Know your wreckage!" evidently was the Branch watchword, and Carstairs seemed to know every aspect of the trade. By the time they boarded the Hercules, he had covered control surfaces, airbrakes, trim tabs, flaps, undercarriage, control settings, fuel cocks, extinguishers, electrical circuitry, hydraulics and a dozen other topics, all in relation to the first basic question: what was the state of the aircraft immediately before its end?

"The public thinks the Black Boxes tell us everything we need to know. They're shifting to flame orange now, by the way, they used to be yellow. But all they tell you is height, airspeed, attitude and compass heading: the newer ones record more parameters, but there's still no substitute for detailed knowledge of your wreckage. The cockpit voice recorders can be helpful, but usually when we turn to them we're looking for pilot error. If the aeroplane was all right before the impact, or was doing something really odd, it helps to know what the pilots *thought* was happening. With single-seat aircraft, you don't even have that advantage: we've just had a US pilot killed on a Harrier conversion course. He was distracted by a jubilee clip which came off an air-hose; and the only reason we know that is because it happened to another pilot, during the transition to hover, but he managed to stay in control..."

In the echoing hold of the cargo aircraft, conversation was more difficult. Pendleton was glad of a pause in the increasingly technical flow of information. Invaluable as it was, the distilled wisdom of a lifetime in air crash investigation, he needed to absorb it in manageable doses. They landed at Benbecula near midnight, still in driving rain, so nothing useful could be done till the morning. Pendleton noticed the smell of the sea as soon as he left the aircraft, a reminder of his Traffic Control days at Prestwick. His billet brought back earlier memories, of his own years in the RAF: but he wasted little time on nostalgia, expecting a long day tomorrow.

Next morning, under grey, driving clouds, he and Carstairs signed out a car from the motor pool and drove down to

Lochboisdale. The road gave them only one view of the sea, from the causeway linking Benbecula to South Uist. Long white breakers rolled in from the west, perhaps bringing more traces of the aircraft for whose loss he would have to account. But first he would have to identify it: nothing had yet been reported missing, and police interest was growing.

"It's not likely to be illegal immigrants, this far north," said Carstairs, as they followed the bumpy road down the island. "But it could be drugs. I had breakfast with the Intelligence Officer, to pick his brains. The Hebrides are one of the routes into the UK, because of the large number of foreign trawlers. Airborne deliveries would be a new trend. But it could be an Intelligence job. The Soviets monitor the rocket range, of course, and the torpedo trials in the Minch, but most of all the nuclear submarines in and out of the Holy Loch. You can hardly see some of their trawlers for the electronic gear they're carrying. But for dropping agents and picking them up, again they work mostly by sea: at most harbours you can just walk off, and there are thousands of beaches and inlets where you can put a boat in. If it was worth the risk of sending in a plane, it could be a major operation."

Sure enough, when they reported to the Police Station, there was a plain-clothes man to escort them to the mortuary. Knowing how few of the islands had even a Special Constable, Pendleton was suitably impressed.

The doctor, a local man, was expecting them to be impressed with the state of the bodies. "You'll be wanting to bring your own pathologists in on this one, I'm thinking," he said as he drew back the sheet.

Pendleton had seen crash effects before, but not like these. "What caused those injuries?" he asked. "Fish?"

Carstairs gave him a scornful look. "We don't have piranha in Scottish waters, Jack. These are wind-blast injuries: supersonic airstream, or near it. That could be consistent with the nakedness: I take it this is how they were found?" The doctor nodded. "Mind you, I'd have expected flying gear to be torn, rather than ripped right off. And we don't have any high-performance aircraft missing...I think the Intelligence chaps are going to be *very* interested in this one."

◈

In that, he was correct. The Soviets were penetrating British airspace at altitude on a regular weekly basis, but with old-fashioned Bear and Bison bombers, testing their Electronic Counter-Measures against far superior systems in which Britain was the world leader. If they had something big which could operate at transonic speed, undetected, that was a very different matter.

By the time Pendleton and Carstairs got back to Benbecula, the rocket range recovery boats had been deployed and Coastal Command was sending a Shackleton from Lossiemouth. These were his decisions, Pendleton realised, actions he could have taken if his investigation warranted it, now taken out of his hands. But at least he was still on the case and had the opportunity to learn.

The old 40's aircraft, "40,000 rivets flying in formation", roared low over the airfield before turning out to sea. Monitoring the search from the control tower, Pendleton and Carstairs marked off the squares of ocean which had been checked. They discussed using trawlers and the local lifeboat, but with the Intelligence aspects so dominating it seemed better to stick with military personnel. Fortunately the area had been closed to shipping for the next series of rocket range firings.

When the results came, they were dramatic.

"Tango George, say again—HOW many bodies floating? Over."

"At least fifteen bodies counted, Tower. A large kidney-shaped fuel slick, large amounts of flotsam. We're dropping chaff for the radar fix on this pass, smoke floats and dye markers for the boats on the next one. Then we'll extend the search pattern downwind, over."

"That's up to twenty bodies so far!" he exclaimed. "It's as if an SST has come apart. What the hell is going on?"

"If it is a supersonic transport, you'll make air crash history," said Carstairs. "You'll be the first Inspector to work on an aircraft type before it's started flight testing—at least in this country. Has anyone checked whether the French Concorde is still in one piece?"

It was intended to be humorous. The first Concorde flight at Toulouse was only three weeks before; the British counterpart, not scheduled till next month. The Soviet Tu-144 had flown at the turn of the year, but little was known about it. It would be madness for either to be carrying such numbers of people, at high Mach, so early in the programmes.

"We have another report from the Shack.," said the Tower operator. "A second slick, ten miles nor-nor-west. More flotsam... ten bodies sighted on first pass...several women, apparently some children..."

"Whatever else it is, it's not military," said Carstairs. "Back to us, till we find out whose it is...Jack, can I make some suggestions?"

"I wish you would!" said Pendleton. "What do we do next?"

"As soon as we get the post-mortem results on the first bodies, we'll know how long they've been in the water. We need to backtrack on currents and surface winds, to try to find the impact points. We can try dropping a line of floats out there, to see how they drift in a corresponding period, but that may not work: it didn't in the '59 Victor investigation. We tried it twice and they all went the wrong ways."

"If we find the main wreckage, can we raise it?"

"You may not need it. With the '67 Comet off Nicosia, we didn't recover from the bottom because it was in 11,000 feet of water, and we were able to determine the cause without it. But at this stage, when you don't even know what *type* of aircraft is involved—and it looks as if someone is covering up—at least you want to know where it is. Normally we'd commission civilian trawlers to make a sonar search, but to keep this thing under wraps, ask for torpedo recovery vessels from the Minch. Royal Navy salvage, too, at least on standby. You may need diving bells, underwater cameras and lifting gear before this is over."

A week later, the Ministry of Defence had made all necessary facilities available and a full security blackout had been imposed. Pendleton and Carstairs briefed the recovery crews on the work of the Branch, the importance of the evidence coming in: Pendleton let Carstairs do most of the talking, because it had to stick to generalities. "Ordinarily, we'd be explaining the investigation in depth. We'd be telling them all about the aircraft, what we know happened to it, what we have to find out. As the reconstruction built up, we'd take them to Farnborough to see it, let them know the value of what they've found and what we're still looking for. And normally, the search team would be a mix of civilian and military. None of that applies this time, either because we don't know the answers at all or because what we know so far doesn't make sense."

With every boat that put back in, the problem worsened. The AIB team was now up to six, though the protocol that Pendleton was in charge was scrupulously observed. All bodies and wreckage had to be documented: sex, age, state and degree of clothing, jewellery etc., position in the water and in the search grid—and for this they were dependent mostly on the coxswains of the recovery vessels, with whom they had to maintain constant liaison. The bodies divided sharply into two groups: the naked ones, badly injured and soaked in fuel, though with no burning, were from the southerly group. The others had apparently floated free after the impact, since injuries were minor. Clothing mostly was disarrayed or detached, implying violent cabin decompression.

One early exception was a young woman of quite extraordinary beauty. Her face had escaped injury, and her expression, unlike

most of the others, was almost ethereally calm. Her body was uninjured, as far as could be told, because it was sheathed in a one-piece garment like a leotard or a body stocking which defied attempts to cut it away.

"It's no fabric I've ever seen," said the flight surgeon. "It's woven, so it allows perspiration—you could take a bath in it and maybe even sunbathe, if you needed that extra protection. And yet it's impervious to the sharpest blades I have. It's as if it's a single, monomolecular fibre. I'd say it was body armour, if it weren't for the colours: they're not exactly military." Though mostly black, the fabric was shot through with kaleidoscopic streaks, blurred by diffraction at the edges.

"Or an all-over chastity belt," said his assistant.

"Well, she doesn't *look* Moslem; and she'd have to be the daughter of a Sheikh or a Maharajah, to make it worth the development cost of something like this."

The flotsam, too, was divided, with inflated life-jackets, personal belongings and fire-extinguishers in the north, cabin furnishings, seat cushions and carpets in the south. This too resembled the 1967 Comet loss, which had been caused by a bomb in the after part of the cabin. Whatever they were after, apparently it had broken apart at altitude and at speed, but a large part of the airframe might be intact.

The search area was extended now over the whole 80 miles to St.Kilda, the most westerly outcrop of the British Isles. Such a long track was unknown in previous AIB experience, but consistent with the near-supersonic airstream to which the southerly bodies had been subjected—provided the initial break-up had been at 30,000 feet or more, in the range of military aircraft like the Canberra. It was a big area to search, but as larger and more recognisable pieces were found the incredible had to be faced.

"The investigation's definitely in your hands now, Jack," said Carstairs. They were in the electronics shack of a submarine salvage vessel, red-lit and filled with the smell of singeing dust and hot solder. On the screen was the flickering picture from a camera

200 feet below. "There's no question whose nationality it is. That's the Union flag, boy, and I don't mean the American north. But I've never seen it shaped into half an arrowhead before. Whose bloody logo is *that*?"

"It could be anyone's," said Pendleton. "Any UK airline, at any rate."

"How so?"

"Because it's perfectly obvious what that is: it's the tail fin of a Concorde. Even though it won't be carrying passengers for years yet, and even though we don't recognise the markings, we have to face it. We've got one, with at least 50 occupants, even before we raise the fuselage from the sea-bed. It's a regular airline flight, we know that from the cabin luggage. On that timescale, any airline can change a livery—BEA's been through three in this decade."

"On that timescale? What the hell d'you mean?"

"Just that we have to accept what we're looking at, however hard it is to believe. The papers and magazines we're fishing out are dated 1999; this aircraft is from the future."

※

"We have a hypothesis before us," said Harrison, the Intelligence captain, "namely, that an aircraft has come back in time. A large volume of alleged evidence has been passed to my department, after drying out and treatment to remove salt and aviation fuel. Much of it has been damaged in the process, and testing its authenticity will now be very difficult."

They were in the office of the Chief Inspector; in London, in Shell-Mex House overlooking the Thames, but without any presence from government or higher levels of the Civil Service—the immunity of the AIB was being upheld, even on this most sensitive issue. Spring had come to England, though not yet to the north: the trees around Farnborough were in leaf, the sun shone outside. The tail-fin on the sea-bed, found only days before the event, was not enough to prevent the British Concorde's maiden flight from Filton; Reginald Turnill had done the commentary, though on the Apollo mission coverage he had been replaced by James Burke. Today's question, crucially, was whether further tests should be suspended and the French government should be informed. With the indications seeming to point to sabotage, and that far in the future, Pendleton had not so far recommended it.

"We have a hypothesis," said Harrison again. "What is the evidence for it? Wreckage, from an aircraft type which is already in existence. Bodies, which could have come from any illicit source. And a large amount of other 'evidence', which I mentioned just now.

"What are the other possible explanations for these? For the first, scrap production components, dumped on the sea-bed under cover of a storm. For the second—people die every day, of causes natural and otherwise. With money, bodies can be obtained—it's no coincidence, I submit, that far too many of these are orientals—and there are wind-tunnels in which blast injuries can be simulated, masking other injuries or causes of death. With time to plan, the most convincing 'victims' can be selected. And for the rest, garbage, as shortly I shall show.

"Who would stand to gain by such a hoax? Opponents of the Concorde programme, on the grounds of cost; enemies of this country, antagonistic to its high-technology success; airlines looking for excuses to cancel options, in a worldwide recession in air travel; environmental groups, anxious to discredit the programme; terrorist groups, wishing to embarrass the government; newspapers fabricating a sensational story. The whole thing could even be some kind of grisly simulation by the manufacturers, who after all are best placed to perpetrate it, if they foresee it going badly wrong in reality. Or more plausibly it could be by their rivals: the American Supersonic Transport programme is a political hot potato, with huge sums involved. And the only one which appears to me to be of any importance is that the Soviets already have their supersonic transport in the air.

"What I have to ask, professionally, is: are these less far-fetched than the future hypothesis? Obviously, the answer is yes. For the hypothesis to survive, the remaining evidence would have to be compelling indeed.

"Instead, as I said before, what we have is garbage—garbage which shows its socialist origins, though some of the devices are subtle. For example: from the literature, we're asked to believe that by the end of this century the Soviet Union has broken up, its member states have capitalist economies, America and Russia are firm friends and in the last stages of scrapping their nuclear arsenals. So there would be no point in building them up now, would there, gentlemen? No need to upgrade Polaris, no need for Chevaline—not that we can use *that* word outside this office. In the immortal words of the Duke of Wellington, if you believe that, you will believe anything.

"Much of the rest of it is more explicit. For example, our national carrier is no longer the British Overseas Airways Corporation, but 'British Airways'—a fine socialist ring that has to it. This is its logo, which you found on the tailplane—here, supposedly, on plastic bags for in-flight off-duty sales. You can find the Union Jack better used in any outfitter's on Carnaby Street. Even the makers' name has been changed: no longer the British Aircraft Corporation, now it's 'British Aerospace'—something else which might appeal to the more extreme back-benchers, and their trade union backers.

"Mr. Pendleton asked us to pay particular attention to the literature concerning the future of spaceflight. Many of the passengers supposedly were going to a conference at the University of Colorado at Boulder, entitled 'The Case for Mars'—4000 miles on a side, with a big handle, I suppose. We have multiple copies of the purported conference programme. Some of the scientists named are real: Professor Carl Sagan and Dr. Brian O'Leary, for example, are genuine experts on the planet Mars, both currently at Cornell University. So I have taken your request to NASA Headquarters in Washington for a summary of current plans.

"There will be at least eleven Moon landings in the first phase, followed by temporary Moon bases and manned mobile laboratories, launched by more advanced versions of the Saturn V booster. There will be two temporary manned space stations called Skylab, followed in 1975 by a semi-permanent 12-man station built by a reusable space plane called the Shuttle. By 1986 there will be 200 Americans in space, 35 of them on or orbiting the Moon and 12 en route to Mars.

"Instead of which, we have here, in a 'potted history of space exploration', that a 4-man station called Freedom (by which I assume they mean Skylab 2) has only just been put up in 1999. Elsewhere it says nevertheless that Skylab 2 is in the 'Smithsonian Air & Space Museum', which is as fictitious as the 'Planetary Society' said to be organising the congress. As for further exploration, it's as if it all stops dead after Apollo 17, only three years from now and in the middle of the current series of missions. Everyone I've spoken to in NASA assures me this is nonsense— wish-fulfilment by the Soviets. They even got a personal statement from Vice-President Spiro Agnew that he'd sacrifice his political career before allowing such a thing to happen.

"However, the Professor Sagan named here is emerging as a critic of the Apollo programme. Dr. O'Leary's position is even stronger: he resigned from astronaut training, with considerable publicity. I'm not so sure that the target of this hoax really is Concorde: it's more as if it's aimed at the American space effort."

"You're speaking now as if you've established that it's a hoax," said the Chief Inspector.

"There are several types of hoax," said Harrison. "There are the successful ones where only the hoaxer knows he's pulled it off; there are the criminal or military ones which have to be successful at the time, but may be revealed later when the purpose has been served. And there are those which have to be revealed almost at once, to embarrass the victims, or to boost the hoaxer's ego. If the object of your 'wreck' is to embarrass the Americans or ourselves, it has to be in that category.

"What we have to look for then—testing my hypothesis now, not yours—are the deliberate absurdities, the things no sane person would have believed, which show what fools the victims are. And that brings us to the 'personal effects' of your corpses. I'll stick to the ones which are plainly absurd or inconsistent.

"1. Contraceptives. Almost everyone over the estimated age of 14 is carrying them, almost all of them condoms—the women as well as the men, and even if they're supposedly on the pill in addition. What's that supposed to imply—some mysterious new sexual disease? Divine vengeance on the permissive society?

"2. Pocket calculators—current market cost just under 400 pounds, for a device which can add, subtract, multiply and divide. Far too many of these people have them, they're too small to be believable, and most of them have functions you can only get on a slide rule or a computer. Arc, sin, cos, tan, roots, reciprocals, in a box you can hold in your hand! Of course, after being subjected to decompression and immersion in salt water, strangely enough we can't find one that works to demonstrate these remarkable properties.

"3. Telephones—on an aircraft!—with push-buttons instead of dials, and funny little aerials instead of wires. Toys, nothing more.

"4. Typewriters—again far too many of them, for any normal planeload of people, let alone Concorde passengers. Whoever they are, I can't see them doing their own typing, let alone on a three-hour flight across the Atlantic! But in any case, most of these things are toys; they don't have any paper in them, or anywhere to feed it in.

"5. Wristwatches. We now have quite a number of them, and they all agree on the time of the crash: but that's a detail any hoaxer would take care of. But most of them don't have hands— just what's supposed to be some kind of digital display. What use would a watch like that be to a Boy Scout? You couldn't even find south with it!"

"If you know the time of day," said the Chief, who was a keen yachtsman, "then you know where the bloody sun is. Stick to the facts, please."

"Very well. There's some other funny stuff—plastic identity cards, issued by banks, for God's sake, not governments, and all with the same funny dark strip on the back. Far too many hearing aids, which apparently could play music tapes if they worked. But the main other point I want to make is about the literature. We don't have any newspapers, which wouldn't be surprising after a storm in the Atlantic, but it would take a lot more imagination to make up a convincing daily newspaper for 30 years hence.

"As for the magazines...! Every crank, idealist political notion you can think of is here. Only one Germany, and yet strategic arms abolition and US withdrawal from Europe are nearing completion. United Europe...common currency—no passports, no trade barriers, *Channel Tunnel tickets*! Japanese electronics! Russian pop stars! 'UK to Have *Second* Woman Prime Minister'! Since there will be no in-flight movies on Concorde, our hoaxers have been spared the trouble of making one specially; but if there had been, I'll bet you it would have been a re-run of some 1960's trash like *Help* or *A Hard Day's Night*. And my reason for saying that is that the in-flight entertainment selection includes the London Symphony Orchestra playing "The Beatles' Classics". Just for the fun of it, I checked that one with a musicologist: apparently there is a chord in *She Loves You*, a flattened seventh or something, which was once used by Beethoven. That'll be the shortest music tape on record. It's utterly unbelievable, Chief Inspector, phoney from start to finish. You're an intelligent man; what's your opinion of the IRA?"

"What—the Irish Republican Army? A spent force, if ever there was one."

"Quite so. Well, according to what this supposed issue of *Time* calls a retrospective, next year—*next year*, mind you—the IRA will be back with a campaign which will bring the British armed forces to an impasse, and then hold the situation in Northern Ireland at that level for more than 20 years. What will end it is the collapse of foreign backing after the Soviet Union turns capitalist and unites with us for a war in the Middle East. As I've said before," said

Harrison, looking pointedly at Pendleton, "if you can believe any of this, you're as crazy as whoever wrote it. You'll believe anything."

"I have to believe the wreckage," said Pendleton. "There's an airliner full of bodies on the floor of the Atlantic, and nothing missing up in the sky. If it's not a Concorde, then what the hell is it?"

"It's a bloody fake, that's what it is. You're the only one here who's even considering anything different."

The Chief said nothing. "Bill?" said Pendleton.

"I have to agree, Jack," said Carstairs, with reluctance. "It's the small details that give it away. Like, these people are all supposedly so wealthy that they haven't a Bank of England pound note between them. In real life, the only people who don't carry small change are the Royal Family. Unless of course you count this dross." He indicated a pile of small coins, like washers, on the table. "You find it in the bottom of handbags, as you'd expect with transatlantic travellers, but the amounts are ridiculous. Take this Chinese-looking thing—'fifty pence'. Who's going to invent a coin worth four-and-tuppence?"

"That's decimalisation," said Pendleton. "It's a year or two off yet, but the Mint's being selling pre-release packs of those coins since last summer."

"Well, if they're on sale, any hoaxer can buy them," Harrison put in. "That's one of many points we checked."

"Be that as it may, what about this thing?" Carstairs held up one of the yellow 'washers'. "These are such poor fakes, the wording isn't even consistent. This dog-Latin on the edge varies from one coin to the next. And it's supposed to be a pound *coin*, in your small change! Do these people buy their drinks ten at a time?"

"In thirty years, that could be inflation," said Pendleton. It got a chorus of protest. "A pound for a *pint*?"

"Another socialist chimera," said Harrison. "The Prime Minister sorted out Robin Day on that one, on Monday night's *Panorama*. Inflation is not a problem in the British economy, and no government—no Conservative government at any rate—will ever take steps to contain it."

"The future never goes the way the experts predict," said Pendleton. "As recently as twelve years ago, Patrick Moore was saying there wouldn't be a Moon landing before 2030; when I was a boy, Professor Low was saying there wouldn't even be a Moon *rocket* for fifty years. For a comparison with what we're facing, I've been looking at a book called *The Dawn of Magic*. One of the authors was a French scientist who spent the war in a prison camp. When he was released and flown back to France, he couldn't believe the equipment on the plane—radar, radio, navigation, all a generation or more ahead of what he'd last seen—and the pilot talking about ballistic missiles and nuclear energy! He compared the experience to time travel, and he'd only been behind the wire for four years."

"'The Dawn of Magic' is about the bloody size of it, if you ask me," said Harrison. He opened his mouth to go on, but the Chief was obviously wearying of the flow of disparagement.

"This is Jack's investigation, and I think it's time to take some decisions. The Minister's waiting to hear from us, Jack: are there grounds to suspend the Concorde programme?"

"I don't think so. If it's genuine, and I think it is, this still looks most like a mid-air explosion, probably a bomb, within the cabin. I do want to go on with retrieval from the sea-bed, at least until we find the flight recorders."

"That's to have full priority, then," said the Chief. "We went through this in 1954, when the Minister resumed commercial Comet flights against the recommendations of the people here. That was before the wreckage was retrieved from the previous crash and the fatigue cracks were found, and it cost another airliner and every soul aboard. I won't have that happen again. If we let Concorde go ahead, even temporarily, then there has to be a total effort to establish the cause of the future accident—or prove it's a hoax.

"Let's suppose for a moment, wild as it seems, that it isn't a hoax. Jack, your only reason for suggesting a bomb is the similarity of the surface debris spread to Comet G-ARCO's. But you don't have any of the evidence we had then for a bomb: nothing the explosives experts can get to work on. And you can't inspect the engines because of the way the wings are lying on the sea-bed. If you're going to grapple them, turn them over for the cameras, then you may as well bring them up, and at that point we're on the way to a full reconstruction of the aircraft. If there's anything else you need, Jack, requisition it; you have the authority, and I'll back you."

Pendleton had digs now in Staines, convenient for both Farnborough and London. Driving home, he pulled off at Virginia Water, to think over the discussion more dispassionately. Whenever he thought about the fake hypothesis, somehow the girl's face came back to his mind. He agreed with the doctor's diagnosis, back under the fluorescents in Lochboisdale: she was from a background of wealth and power, in which she was protected and probably loved. Even if her porous 'armour' could be manufactured today, and he was still waiting for the ICI chemists' verdict on that, and if she had died from natural causes, could anyone bear to let her be dumped at night in the Atlantic, miles from land, on the offchance that she'd be found—and if so, remain unburied? None of the bodies could be laid to rest until this mystery was solved. And the other possibilities Harrison had hinted at: deliberate murder and experiment, building up a stock of suitably convincing 'victims'—for someone like her, the thought was not seriously to be considered.

The pub was old-style, the way he liked them, still with hand-pulled beer in an age of plastic pumps and metal kegs. There was a new addition, though: a colour television, incongruous above the end of the bar. The landlord had been talking about it, in anticipation of the Moon landing, with a late license for his regulars. The evening News was on, as he slipped on to a bar-stool to savour his pint.

"...Crowds of screaming fans surrounded Marylebone Police Court today, and several fans were arrested after clashes with the police, when Mick Jagger and Marianne Faithfull appeared to answer charges of possessing cannabis resin. Their appearance in court was brief, and a trial date was set for January.

"The Apollo 10 astronauts, now en route to the Moon, gave a TV broadcast earlier today in which they demonstrated equipment they will use, on the last space mission before the Moon landing in July..."

Cannabis resin? Could that explain the girl's unnatural calm, when she must have had *some* indication of the break-up of the aircraft? Already there were long-haired intellectuals saying the stuff should be legalised. In thirty years, maybe...but the thought of pot fumes in the air-circulation of a supersonic airliner was enough to give any pilot the hab-dabs.

"That's not possible," said the man at his elbow. It was disconcerting, as if his mind had been read.

"Beg pardon?"

"That," said the man, pointing at the screen. "Up till now I thought they were idiots, those people who say it's all being done in a TV studio. But I can't believe that."

"Why, what's wrong with it?" It had looked like a re-run of Apollo 8 so far, though now the camera was going through into the Lunar Module.

"That demonstration he's just given of the onboard computer. Listen, I'm a Systems Analyst, I trained as a programmer with IBM. I can't get performance like that out of my company's mainframe, and he's saying he can get it from a box the size of a small typewriter!"

It was the second time that day he had heard the comparison. But if every businessman could have the equivalent of a mainframe in his lap; and a cordless phone—through satellites?—so that he could stay in touch with the office, then why burden himself with paper? Himself, or herself, since the women had them too. And if there was a revolution in business equality, why not in sexuality? Harrison's list of 'impossibilities' might be long, but if he could believe any of them he could believe them all. The Concorde in the Hebrides was no hoax, and he saw what his responsibility now would have to be.

⬦

The recovery crews, now, were all picked men, and the Intelligence presence was everywhere. They were lucky that the impacts had been west of the Uists, where the first bodies were spotted on the long beaches in time for the rest to be intercepted at sea. Had it been over the Minch, they might not have been found among the inlets of West Skye—not at least until so much had come ashore that the secret could never be kept. As it was, with so much retrieval going on out there and with no aircraft reported missing, the operation passed unnoticed.

Of course, they couldn't find everything. Enough was found by other people, and was strange enough, to set tongues wagging on both sides of the Minch. *The West Highland Free Press* flew the occasional kite; 'Bodies But No Murder' was one of their more accurate headlines, had they known it. But the Ministry line remained firm. "Nothing missing. Rumours? No comment." *Private Eye* got on to it, trying to link the rumours to their campaign about the Aer Lingus Viscount lost off the Royal Aircraft Establishment's own rocket range at Aberporth the previous year. But not even the satirical journal, fighting its way from lawsuit to lawsuit, could make anything of an RAE refusal to answer questions when no aircraft was missing at all.

If the reconstruction had been at Filton, the wreckage could be compared with actual aircraft complete or under construction; but that was out of the question. Instead the RAE Structures Department turned over still another hangar, T-50, where the operation could proceed in secret. A major airlift was organised to bring the wreckage to Farnborough, using everything from Beverleys to Herons, with everything shrouded in plastic or canvas to conceal it from the air and ground crews. The tang of the Hebridean sea came to the Accidents Section, the reconstruction hangar, labs and some of the offices smelling like the quay of a fishing port.

It was especially odd to be commuting from the Hebrides to Farnborough, in these circumstances. The contrast between the flat, near-treeless islands and the leafy lanes of Hampshire was startling enough; and then of course the difference in temperature; but most of all the sky. In Scotland in June and July, especially in the north, twilight lasted all night unless hidden by clouds; in the south of England, the sky was jet black and the stars were brilliant, all the way down to the horizon, not even hidden by the Hebridean haze. He could walk out of the sea-smelling hangar, let his eyes adjust, and see the Milky Way and the Andromeda Nebula— invisible, at this time of year, where those smells belonged.

The tail section, with its puzzling logo, was among the first to be raised. "I don't believe *that* at all," said Carstairs, pointing to the registration number.

"G-BOAG—what's the matter with that?"

"You'd know if you were from civil aviation, instead of military. BOAC use the letters G-BOAC on every piece of promotional artwork, for every aircraft type. It drives plane spotters mad because they can't tell whether the illustration shows a real aeroplane. And that reg. isn't different enough to be plausible."

As the sorting out began, allocating pieces to their positions on the chalk diagram and the rising wooden frames, a list of part numbers began to be compiled. Discreet enquiries at Filton established that they were later in the production series than for any aircraft built yet. Confirmation that production would continue would have been welcome to the workforce there, worried about their jobs: the campaign against Concorde was continuing, prominently featuring Mary Goldring of the *Observer*, and Members of Parliament raised Cain in the House when it was announced that costs were already 62% higher than the last estimate of 450 million pounds, just three years before.

Leeds United won the F.A. Cup; Blakeney won the Derby. England, led by Boycott and Illingworth against the West Indies in the Test, drew the second match but won the first and third. Graham Hill won the Monaco Grand Prix, Jackie Stewart the French and the British. John Fairfax completed his transatlantic row; and John Pendleton found the ghost Concorde's flight recorders.

One of his fears had been that he might not be able to read them. But changing the flight data recorder system on an aircraft was what the Navy would term a 'dockyard job', a major redesign of key features. There were still many aircraft flying with the original foil recorders, some of the longer production runs with aircraft younger than the instruments they'd been built around. At the end of the century, there would still be machines with present-day tape or wire recorders: the ones off this Concorde were the very newest, for Pendleton's time, but they could be read.

It had been at 40,000 feet, climbing, the four Olympus engines running smoothly. They already knew that, though it had meant raising the wings: otherwise they might not have bothered, since Concorde had no flaps or leading edge slats for study and the positions of the main control surfaces were obvious. The nose-cone had been found, having snapped off on impact with the water, and study of the hinges showed that it had been correctly raised to shield the cockpit windows in flight. All the major parts were now in place on the wooden frames, along with many smaller pieces of the framework and skin. It looked as if it had been attacked by metal-eating moths, rather than torn apart and painstakingly re-assembled. Nevertheless, since the wheels were up, from many angles it seemed to be skimming low over the hangar floor in ghostly flight. At least with the bodies in cold storage, the most macabre aspect was being avoided: they couldn't be buried legally without a coroner's verdict, and in these circumstances that kind of enquiry was to be avoided at all costs.

As it crossed South Uist the machine had still been travelling below Mach One: it implied that supersonic flight over populated areas had not been licensed, and if he could only make that known, the entire planned series of acceptability tests down the west coast of Britain could be dispensed with. But as to the crash, nothing new was learned: the sudden break in the recording supported the sabotage hypothesis, because a bomb in an aircraft normally cuts off electrical power.

The same applied to the cockpit voice recorder. "The only odd thing," he told Carstairs, "is that overflying Air Traffic Control is from something called Atlantic House, not Redbrae, and there aren't any bearings given on Western Gailes. They *are* using a navigation system called GPS, which is a new one on me."

"And the voice quality?"

"Perfectly clear—as if they're using more channels, in fact."

As the reconstruction continued, the sequence of events became clearer. 'Trajectory planning', the technique the AIB had pioneered to reconstruct the breakup of machines in the air from the fall of the debris, was already a very powerful tool (especially since it came into play *after* the flight data recorder ceased to operate): but allied to the new generation of mainframe computers now available, even if they lacked the powers of the one on Apollo and the everyday ones on the Concorde, they were not only powerful but swift. It was a strange thought that if any of those so-called 'typewriters' was what it appeared to be, and still been working, it might have solved the problem without even the man- and machine-hours of the 'new' methods.

Still, brilliant things had been done before such aids were available. In the Comet wreckage of 1954, a cabin paint fleck on the wing and an Indian coin embedded in the tail showed that the cabin had ruptured first. The bomb on Comet G-ARCO had been deduced from the examination of just 27 recovered seat cushions: the Chief Inspector had, by chance, recognised a similarity to a cushion used a a muffler in a safe-breaking incident. In a detailed study by the Royal Armament Research and Development

Establishment, the position of the bomb was determined to within half an inch; without computers, at any stage, and without recovering the aircraft from depth.

By comparison, Pendleton had an *embarras de richesse*: the increasing amounts of recovered wreckage, the flight recorders, more material coming to hand by the day. What he didn't have, unfortunately, was explosion traces in the ordinary sense. It was now clear that the aircraft had come apart between the wings, forward of the engine nozzles. The skin had peeled back as far as the fin and the forepart went into an irretrievable spin as it began to decelerate. But everything located, from either section, made it seem that the missing ribs of the airframe had simply evaporated: a moment there, then gone, with the decompression and the slipstream combining to shred everything in their path before turning back, a fraction of a second later, to attack the people and things forward of the break. Every fragment found embedded in soft material was from the aircraft itself, driven by the hurricane-force of the decompression.

So it wasn't a bomb: more like something science-fictional, a disintegrator or a matter-transmitter. The much-delayed commencement of *Star Trek* on the BBC just at this time could scarcely have been less convenient. But whatever had happened out there was outside normal experience, if only for the first fraction of a second. And it was, irremovably, by Act of Parliament, his to investigate.

As the year wore on, the finds of wreckage and bodies petered out. Every so often, however, the beaches would yield another oddity, painstakingly to be added to the vast jigsaw of metal and paperwork. It was unnerving, how much of the aircraft had now taken shape in the reconstruction. 70% of the 1959 Victor had been recovered, in 592,610 pieces, using 40 ships and 1500 men; 80% of the 1954 Comet had been found, using more basic techniques but in more friendly waters. In rough but shallow sea, his retrieval was approaching the same proportions. With each new find, Pendleton would stand down from the readiness rota for a day or a week, however long it took to fit the new piece into place. The rest of the time, plastic sheets were spread over it, as protection from the inevitable leaks in the hangar roof—making it seem like some brand-new, secret prototype, rather than an airliner well through its operational life.

In any other investigation, by now the wreckage would be boxed away, out in the AIB compound, waiting for Lloyd's or the Ministry of Defence to decide on its disposal. There was no argument about it, but it was a big problem for the Branch to leave it in the hangar, under guard, for what could be a long time indeed.

Otherwise, his training in Air Accident investigation had been resumed, at the beginning, as it had to be. The Concorde investigation had landed in his lap only by chance: perhaps because it was so weird and politically such a hot potato that nobody else wanted it, but ostensibly because of the written rules and the unwritten protocols, nobody ever suggested his removal. He often considered giving it up, knowing how big it already was and how much bigger it was liable to get before it was over; but each time, his personal responsibility, and the face of the girl—a symbol, already, of all the occupants of the aeroplane—kept him from putting pen to paper.

So he worked on light aircraft, then executive aircraft, and single-seat military models—trainers, then combat types he had flown, then the newer marks. He came to know the other distinctive smells of crash sites: not just the ubiquitous kerosine, and sometimes the reek of burning, but the wrongly, wrongly, clean smell of freshly broken pine which came to evoke all crashes, or so he was told. With it, too, came recognition of that "inner sense of elation—a sort of tingling and excitement" when the cause of an accident was found; the charge which the hidden Concorde had still to yield to him.

As an Operations Inspector, he would have to qualify and remain current on at least one large public transport aircraft, plus club and private licenses which he already had. He couldn't start on Concorde, obviously, since it was still in flight testing; but with the intimate knowledge of the aircraft which he now had, even if much of it couldn't be acknowledged on his dossier, he would be in its left-hand seat in due course. He would never have flown at that speed if he had stayed in the Royal Air Force, though if he'd gone into flight testing he might have done some of the things with Lightnings that nobody talked about on the record. Officially, because of the cancelled projects of the '60's, Britain's front-line fighters still couldn't intercept the country's flagship civil airliner.

When he switched on the lights in Hangar T-50 after weeks away from it, the first sight of the reconstruction hanging in its frame always came as a shock. Sometimes it lived in his dreams, trying to tell him the answer in voices he could never quite make out—the pilots, whose voices he knew from the cockpit tape; the girl; or a rasping, mechanical voice of its own.

The guards had been withdrawn from the hangar, to avoid drawing attention to it: on an airfield with restricted access, locked doors and a sign saying "High voltage—keep out" were an adequate deterrent to curiosity. Pendleton had considered a variety of other official signs, including "Radioactive Material" or "Lasers in Use", with the appropriate symbols, or something sinister about protective clothing with a skull-and-crossbones, from the biological warfare establishment at Porton Down; but he wanted the put-off to be as mundane as possible, not even worth mentioning in the pub.

In that, he wasn't entirely successful. In 1972 the *Daily Mirror* ran a front-page story alleging that the RAF had a crashed UFO in Hangar T-50. A live extraterrestrial was supposed to have been seen with the Prime Minister, visiting Her Majesty at Balmoral. Guards had to be posted again, to keep away Flying Saucer fanatics who were nearer the truth than they realised. The Defence

Correspondent of *The Times* opined that most probably the wreck within was of some classified military hardware, possibly a Remotely Piloted Vehicle for battlefield reconnaissance, and the story gradually faded. At least, from now on, enquiries could be laughed off.

The problem with Concorde G-BOAG, after all, was that it was all too clearly identified; and the government didn't want *that* becoming known. As costs rose to five times the original estimates Tony Benn, now Minister for Technology, was trying to have Concorde scrapped, turned into high-tech jewellery and ashtrays like the components of Blue Streak and TSR2. Pan Am, then the world leader, had turned against the aircraft in 1970, and the other sixteen airlines with options were holding back. A revelation like this was the last thing Benn wanted: it would be overkill, promptly denounced by the Opposition as a vastly expensive trick. However, the Conservatives in 1962 had sewn up the agreements far too strongly for cancellation, to make sure the *French* could not back out; there was a prospect of a back-bench rebellion in parliament, with 250,000 jobs at stake at Filton and Toulouse; so it was convenient to accept the serious warnings by government scientists on the unknowable effects of preventing the accident at this stage.

Instead it was to be forgotten—if it had come from the 1990's, let the 1990's take care of it. Prince Philip took Concorde's controls in May, and in June the plane paced an eclipse of the Sun across Africa. Late in the year, the boards of BOAC and British European Airways were merged into the new 'British Airways'— and President Nixon cancelled the Apollo programme, putting two million people out of work and starting a recession which was blamed on the Arabs.

Registration numbers were allocated to the new aircraft. A nice in-joke had been perpetrated: they began with G-BOAA, at once known to aviation correspondents as 'Double Alpha', and continued in sequence. So there was a G-BOAC, at last, and would be a BOAG in due course. The first mysteries had been resolved, the jigsaw became a little more complete. But the oil crisis did hurt Concorde: it was becoming clear, now, that the sixteen aircraft taken by British Airways and Air France would be all the orders there were.

For the Accident Investigation Branch, there was plenty of other work on hand. A series of battles had developed with the American Federal Aviation Administration over the implementation of safety recommendations. The Paris DC-10 crash killing 346, the worst air accident to date, involved heavy British casualties and brought the issue to a head, while public attention was focussed on the discrepancy in compensation awarded by British and American courts.

In that and other accidents with wide-bodied jets, the loss of life was much greater than in the Concorde—which after all in a sense was still to happen. Tenerife, when it came, was worst of all. But in his dreams the shadowy Concorde remained the priority, the girl now the only passenger whose face he could recall. Knowing that she was still unburied in death, not yet conceived in life, he was haunted by her and relations with other women did not succeed. Was he obsessed? he often wondered. Not in a way that impaired his work, at any rate, and the better he was at that, the more likely he was to succeed in the task he had set himself.

In 1977 British Aerospace, too, became a reality, sweeping up not just the British Aircraft Corporation but all the remaining grand names of British aviation: Hawker Siddley, Avro, Vickers, Handley Page, English Electric and even Scottish Aviation Limited, whose initials his friends at Prestwick told him now stood for 'Saved At Last'.

In the same year, Concorde began passenger services to New York. The development costs had been written off, and British Airways had in the end received its eight aircraft without payment; but the project had cost the taxpayer nine hundred million pounds. In 1981, the parliamentary Industry and Trade Committee called for an end to subsidy of Concorde. Far from scrapping its flagship, the government's response was to allocate another 123 million to operations over the next five years; in that context, even a mention of what was in Hangar T-50 could be construed as an attack on government policy, and Mrs. Thatcher would be having none of *that*, thank you very much.

"...But Mr. Pendleton," said the Prime Minister in deep, earnest tones, as if talking to a child, "what you fail to realise is that Britain must have fully independent capability to destroy the USSR. Whether we will do so, or whether it will destroy itself, is not really relevant. What matters for our prestige and sovereignty is that we *can*. What your Royal Air Force colleagues fail to recognise is that the systems they backed—the V-bombers with Blue Steel, TSR-2, all the British-built, manned forms of deterrent—would have failed to give us sufficient destructive power. Buying Skybolt or the F-111 from the United States were only steps on the way. What successive British governments really wanted was Polaris, because when it is obsolescent Polaris will lead to Trident."

She paused, expectantly, for him to ask the reasons. Pendleton realised that because he was in possession of one major secret, he was being tested on his worthiness to share others. He refused to be drawn: there had been, as far as he knew, no update of Harrison's report, which had dismissed the possibility of a UK woman Prime Minister—as Mrs. Thatcher herself had, around the same time. Pendleton had known she would make it—he had won a bet on it. But he knew and she didn't what her political fate was to be. It would be a long run, but it would end long before 1999, and to accomplish what he had to accomplish he couldn't go down with her.

"The point, Mr. Pendleton," she went on, when he said nothing, "is that the national interest involves issues, much bigger issues, than the scientific paradoxes raised by the Concorde wreckage. It is not to be discussed, not to be discussed at all."

The rest of the inner Cabinet were nodding emphatically. With Norman Tebbitt, looming at the end of the table, about to approve the AIB's long-delayed office move to Farnborough, it had been quite strongly suggested to Pendleton that these people should not be antagonised unless the integrity of the Branch was at stake.

"Why is the new pound coin called a Thatcher?" asked Neil Kinnock, at the Labour Party Conference. "Because it's thick and brassy, and believes it's a sovereign..." Much more important, to Pendleton, was that another piece of 'funny money' had been explained and the Bank of England pound note would be withdrawn. In the same year, on a visit to London, he found in the street an IBM conference folder which the attendee had casually thrown away—including the complimentary scientific calculator inside, not worth retaining. He went to see Carstairs in retirement, and they had a drink on the strength of it.

By the time Thatcher, too, was gone, the Cold War was truly ending. Pendleton found himself called upon to brief the new inner Cabinet, and the investigation took on a new danger: after a government which didn't want to know about the Concorde, and another which ignored it, now there was one which wanted to mine it of information and profit by it.

"I'm against tracing of any kind," he told Maitland, a whizz-kid scientist who'd been assigned to him from Harwell. "Harrison and his people checked passports, driving licences and the rest back in the early '70's. They found some people existed, all much younger, as you'd expect; some they couldn't find, some hadn't been born yet. But the scientists we brought in at that time advised against the whole exercise. The closer we get to 1999, the more visible these people will become. Many of them will be VIP's. In the last year before the crash, the passenger list will start filling up." Now that Concorde was profitable, 'from white elephant to golden eagle' with its fan club and its dedicated passengers, seats were booked months in advance and people became irrationally attached to their places, insisting on the same number for every flight. "That information should be kept away from government. If too many people know, find out they or their friends are on the list and cancel the bookings, God knows what will happen. At the very least, there could be so many changes that we never figure out what happens."

"What if it's the Prime Minister of the day?" said Maitland. "Might depend on your politics, I suppose..."

"We do what we're going to do anyway," said Pendleton. "*We prevent it from happening.*"

And that made it explicit: the purpose which had directed his life, now for more than twenty years. So often in his work, he had been so close in imagination to those last moments in the cockpit that it seemed he could reach in and tap the pilot on the shoulder. "Wires—you're too low! Go round again!" "Number Three's going to windmill—feather it now!" But it was never possible: you could only try to make sure it never happened again, whatever it was. Knowing that the interacting complexities of the machines, the sky and the human pilot would be sure to come up with a new one...but worse was when you found out, and you issued the warning, and it happened again anyway.

From the cockpit voice recorders, those voices—"We've lost it," from the Turkish DC-10; that German hero, describing everything he was doing to pull out, ending "Well, goodbye, everybody..."; from the *Challenger*, that incredibly restrained "Uh-oh"; but most often, sometimes in trepidation, seldom in fear, that final and heartfelt, "Oh, shit." And now, for the first time ever, the chance to prevent one: to intervene at the crucial moment in an accident because in a sense, it hadn't happened yet.

If only—on the day itself, if it came to that—he could figure out what 'it' was.

※

And now at last it was the day: June 30th, 1999, a date which he had been anticipating for thirty years. He had wondered, in the years when he carried the secret almost alone, what would happen if some accident had taken him out before the day arrived. Would the wreckage have been disposed of, or simply sealed up in Hangar T-50, until whatever was about to happen had taken its course? His rise in status in the '90's had at least made sure that there would be preparations—whether they were adequate remained to be seen.

The barriers to promotion had been removed, as Maitland and his team made clear the magnitude of the secret he had kept, and the potential risks if he had allowed the investigation either to be terminated or made public. He had made Senior Inspector in 1988, after participating in the British Airways strip-down of Concorde 'Double Alpha' at Heathrow. That enquiry found the airliners fit to continue flying into next century. Ironically, Pendleton could have told them that, because the exercise reversed the painstaking re-assembly of G-BOAG nineteen years before. In 1992, part of the rudder was lost at 56,000 feet; two previous incidents had been traced to paint stripper corrosion, but the more rigorous investigation of the third one brought him up to Assistant Principal. He was a Principal Inspector now, with thirty years' seniority, and in the run-up to this day he had used all the powers which the old Chief Inspector had conferred on him when he was put in charge of the investigation.

And still he didn't know what he was looking for! That crucial area of cabin, forward of the engine nozzles, was still simply missing, without fragments or chemical traces on the rest to reveal what had happened to it. By ill luck, hardly any of those seats had been pre-booked; for those which had, the occupants had been thoroughly vetted and seemed to be clean. The remaining seats would go to late arrivals, mostly businessmen in a hurry, and were being allocated as boarding passes were handed out at the entrance to the departure lounge. As they were, hidden security cameras scanned them and the National Remote Sensing Centre (also at Farnborough, by good fortune) was profiling and matching them with the dead who had been recovered.

At New Scotland Yard, a similar exercise was matching them against known terrorists and criminals, as fast as could be done with those much more extensive files to search. In the lounge itself, Special Branch and Intelligence officers were mingling with the passengers, marking out each person they *didn't* recognise from the Identikit pictures they had been required to memorise. For Pendleton it was more bizarre to recognise so many, just the ages they had been when fished from the sea thirty years ago. He had to restrain the automatic social impulse to greet them as acquaintances.

The officers had not been briefed on the true nature of the enquiry. The risk of interference with the course of events was too great. With the passing years, Maitland and his colleagues had grown stronger in their warnings of the threat to reality, unless flight BA-002 remained closely in parallel with its past and future counterpart.

But with them knowing so little, the surveillance might be misdirected. They thought they knew what they were looking for, and although they had been briefed to look for *anything* unusual, anything at all, they might miss something vital.

And if they did, or if there was nothing detectable in any case, then after boarding the departure would be placed on hold. Pendleton would phone Downing Street and repeat his earlier recommendation to cancel the flight. As he saw it, his duty was clear. Maitland would then take the phone and, presumably, repeat *his* earlier recommendation that it go ahead, almost certainly sacrificing airliner, passengers and crew to avoid any risk that causality would be violated.

It would be the Prime Minister's personal decision. And if it went against him, what then? He knew a Rolls-Royce engineer who had once, as an apprentice, physically stopped a Tristar from departing a Middle East airport because he'd seen the carbon fibre blades of its RB-211 engines being mistreated. It had been only slightly less dramatic than the undercarriage incident in Nevil Shute's *No Highway*. But neither the fictitious hero nor the real one had been surrounded by armed security, ready to jump on anyone whose actions were in any way unusual.

Ominously, the Concorde in Hangar T-50 had been briefly delayed. Takeoff was scheduled at 1100 hours, to have the passengers in New York for lunch. The flight plan did indeed cross the Hebrides, going north of the transatlantic great circle route and coming down over Labrador instead of Newfoundland. But travelling subsonically over land, the Concorde would overfly South Uist at 11.50. According to the flight recorders and the watches of the occupants, breakup had been at seven minutes past midday; so takeoff had been delayed about fifteen minutes and presumably would be again.

"Good morning, ladies and gentlemen. British Airways Concorde flight BA-002 to New York is now boarding. Will all passengers with seats in rows 1 to 14 please make their way to the departure gate at the end of the Lounge..."

"I think we have your men, sir," said a Special Branch officer at his elbow. "Three Arab gentlemen, travelling in the after part of the Business Section with cabin luggage, just getting up now although their seat numbers haven't been called yet. We've traced their movements in the last few days to Libya, via the Middle East and Germany. It's Lockerbie all over again."

"Go ahead, then. A full search, personal as well as luggage. Apologies if you find nothing, but their flight bags are *not* to be returned to them before they board the aircraft."

Plain-clothes men moved in. "Could you come this way, sir? Just a small query, purely routine..." The Arabs seemed puzzled, but went along without objection. Of course, they wouldn't want to attract attention, or might not know what they were carrying.

Could that be all? Could it be so easy? There had been a decline in international terrorism, especially against the airlines. He had been expecting something much more exotic, some lone-wolf inventor, an extraterrestrial or even a time-traveller! Was his lack of reaction just disappointment at something so mundane? On the other hand, he had yet to hear what kind of extraordinary terrorist device this might be.

One way or the other, the 'electric thrill' had so far failed to possess him, as the first group of passengers filed into the tunnel leading to the aircraft. The feeling of *deja vu* was bizarre: he could sympathise with Maitland's fears that reality itself was under threat.

Just in front of him, three men turned to wave to a colleague. They must have booked very late, to have to be allocated seats in different parts of the aircraft—and that put the other at the back of Business Class, right in the danger area. Two of these at least he recognised. The man still seated was a stranger; short, with glasses, nondescriptly dressed for a Concorde passenger. As he settled back his briefcase caught on the rim of his seat, revealing that it was fastened to his wrist.

Could it be...? To Pendleton's hyped-up sensibilities, it seemed at least possible. Forcing himself to act casually, he walked across, dropping into a seat the boarding colleagues had vacated.

"Excuse me, sir, may I ask you—what are you carrying in that case?"

If the Arabs had been too casual, this was an over-reaction. "What do you mean? What business is that of yours?"

Pendleton showed his identity card—not that this man, with his thick accent (Russian? Ukrainian?) was likely to recognise it. "It's an official matter, sir, just a routine enquiry. Can you tell me what you are carrying?"

"I answered all questions at the check-in!" The man seemed suspicious, rather than alarmed, but his response was decidedly abnormal. "I have nothing further to say."

No, definitely not right. "I'm afraid I must insist, sir. Please come with me."

"I will not—!" But time was running out. Pendleton signalled to two security men, and as the lounge emptied they seized his suspect by the arms, lifting him out of his seat.

As Pendleton rose to follow, he was passed by the girl. She strolled casually through from the bar, smartly dressed in black— no hint of the swirling colours below. Her beauty made everyone else in the room seem drab, and it was doubly startling to see her in motion, as if the corpse he had seen in Lochboisdale so long ago had sprung off the table and into life. And still he had no idea who she was: she wasn't a model or a film star after all, for he had never found her in glossy magazines or tabloids, and he had looked often enough.

She looked right through him, and irrationally that was hurtful; as if she could know how she had haunted him, hopelessly, all these years. If she noticed Jack Pendleton, Principal Inspector, it was as a balding 60-year-old, slightly pot-bellied as a result of his loyalty to traditional beer; probably an airport official, since he wasn't boarding the plane. It wouldn't cross her mind that he could do anything for her, much less the enormous service he was trying to render, on which there was no time even to watch her go.

"This is outrageous!" the man was protesting, as he caught up with him in the side room. "I am Oleg Kerowski of the Russian Academy of Sciences! I demand to join my colleagues on the aircraft, otherwise my government shall hear of this without delay!"

"You're not being abducted, sir, not in the ordinary sense. This is a matter not just of security, more even than national security. It is one of life or death. I must ask you again what is in your case."

"Very well! It is a sample of a crystal material from Phobos, the satellite of Mars, which was returned by our space probe last year."

'By Christ', as a predecessor had said, 'this must be it'. The feeling of certainty descended on him. "Are you then going to the Case for Mars conference in Boulder, Colorado?"

"Yes—how would you know? The sample has been in Europe for diffraction-pattern study by high-energy particle beam, at CERN. Now I am taking it to the United States, as provided for by the international cooperation on the mission. We have avoided publicity for all this, so that elaborate security precautions would not be necessary. Why do you intervene?"

"There's no time to explain, sir. But under no circumstances can I allow that crystal to go aboard the aircraft. This is Professor Alan Maitland, of Harwell, whom I think you must know by reputation. I hope he can persuade you of our need for your cooperation." Kerowski looked surprised, but appeared to recognise Maitland when he looked at him again.

"I have to disagree with Mr. Pendleton on the wisdom of this course," said Maitland. Seven years on, he had acquired a gravity far removed from his earlier image. "But it seems likely that the particle beam has changed the composition of your sample. If it remains here, we may be able to get some measure of that. I can confirm that if you took the crystal aboard the Concorde all of your lives would be forfeit."

"How could you know that?" said Kerowski. "I will not release the case. I must warn you, there are bio-sensors in the wrist band. Security devices will be activated if it is removed without my authorisation."

"In that case, you may not board the aircraft," Pendleton replied. "I have the powers to insist that you come with us, and when you see the evidence that we have, I hope you will change your mind."

Like it or not, Kerowski was escorted from the terminal at a fast pace, the security officers urged on by Pendleton and Maitland. At the side of the building a jet helicopter was waiting, and as arranged the pilot started up as soon as they appeared. Despite their priority, they had to wait briefly for clearance, and as they took off, he noticed with concern that Concorde G-BOAG had been cleared to taxi.

"The Prime Minister is on the radio, sir." Pendleton had not waited to make the arranged call, and that had to be made good with a link-up through the Heathrow control tower. "I believe we have the answer," Pendleton reported. "Given that, I now agree with Professor Maitland. The flight should go ahead, to keep the sequence of events as closely linked as possible. The danger now is here, not in the air."

"This is all very theatrical," said Kerowski. "Am I to believe that conversation was genuine?"

"When you see what we have to show you, I think you will." As they flew on, Maitland tried to explain. Pendleton had a house in

Staines, now: they were crossing the motorway junction on which he was caught in a tailback, four mornings out of five. To the helicopter it was an easy hop. Still, time was slipping away: behind them, G-BOAG was already in the air.

It was a still day, slightly misty, as if nature itself was waiting for the mystery to be resolved. As they came in over Farnborough's famous Black Sheds, Pendleton was reminded of his first day here and the history of the place. One way or another, in a few minutes it would alter again.

They landed by the AAIB headquarters, the rotors still turning as they left the machine. This too was pre-arranged: it wasn't likely there would be time to get away, if things went badly wrong, but the pilot had volunteered. Another brisk march followed, over to Hangar T-50 and the waiting wreck of the airliner, still poised as if in flight like its counterpart, now nearing the Borders.

Kerowski had stopped in his tracks, then stepped forward to stare at the aircraft from a different angle. "It's impressive, but you could have staged it."

"What—all of this, just to get you to let go of that case? Besides, even a brief inspection will show you the airstream and water damage. We couldn't have lost a real Concorde and kept that secret."

That got a sad nod. "We lost our SST in 1973, at the Paris Air Show. I had a part in the calculations for that project..."

"One more thing may convince you, sir. Please come this way—there's very little time."

He led the Russian across the hangar floor, towards the crucial anomaly—the lettering, below the cockpit windows, which fortunately had survived the detachment of the nose cone. "We have followed the counterpart of this aircraft through its history, through construction and testing, into service, waiting for the flight in which all the details matched. Between this aircraft, and the one in the air, this is the only point of difference."

"I see nothing significant," said Kerowski.

"It's the name, sir. Concorde doesn't have its name on it, because all the world knows what it is. Yet it would have had, but for a political gesture.

"The original plan was for the Concordes completed in France to have the final 'e', while those finished here would be 'Concord', as you see it. It was Tony Benn, afterwards an opponent of the project, who announced the change in 1967. At the roll-out of Sud-Aviation's prototype he announced that all Concordes would have the final 'e', to stand for entente, excellence and England."

He had Kerowski's full attention, but still he hadn't conveyed his point. "*This isn't our Concorde.* It's from a different universe, one differing from ours only by a government Minister's decision on the name of an aircraft. Somehow your crystal linked those universes, pushing this 'Concord' into ours and thirty years into the past. It doesn't belong here, and we have to send it back."

"You have a poetic way of putting things, Mr. Pendleton," said Kerowski. "You should have been a physicist." With that, he drew out a pen, touched its point to the bracelet at several points, and handed Pendleton the case as it came free from his wrist.

"Thank you, sir—good God!" He had looked at his watch—digital, of course!—and found its reading frighteningly close to the one on all those other watches, inside. "Get him out of here! Either the control room or the chopper—but you two get in the chopper and get out altogether."

He strode down the aircraft, up the ladder and along the wing. Ducking in through the breach in the fuselage, he was confronted by the evidence he hadn't had to show. The recovered bodies were back in their seats, the last of them matched up with the boarding list relayed from Heathrow; thawing out, after thirty years, but still with a glossy sheen of frost. He couldn't have shown Kerowski his own body, blown to bits, presumably, in the other universe, but his colleagues were here.

Most bodies had major injuries; some had been days or weeks in the water before being picked up; some had been subjected to post-mortem dissection. Viewed one by one, in the antiseptic chill of the mortuary, they could be treated with professional detachment. Collectively, here, they made a scene from a horror movie.

He forced himself not to look towards the girl's place, as he matched up Kerowski's seat number and fastened the briefcase to the frame. Better, far better to remember her as he had seen her minutes ago, remote but wholly alive. At least now the crystal was here with the wreck, and not with those people up there.

At the side door, despite the need to get clear, he paused for a last look. This time, the lights had to stay on, but there was no reason to believe he would ever see his reconstruction again. He closed the door, and walked briskly to the Admin block; it would be undignified to run.

Kerowski had opted for the control room, and was there with Maitland. Screens showed the wreckage from every possible angle, and in many different frequencies: proximity to the Remote Sensing Centre had again been an advantage. "Have you evacuated everyone else?" the Russian asked.

"We don't know how much energy will be channelled through the crystal at the crucial moment," said Pendleton. "If it's $E=MC^2$, for the whole mass of the aircraft, then we should have evacuated most of western Europe! It'll be one hell of a bang. There was talk of getting the wreckage off the Earth's surface, but we can't orbit a whole airliner even today. We might have asked you to do it with an Energia, if we melted it or crushed it and sent it up in blocks, but then the identity question would have arisen—it's the organisation of the matter which characterises it as the plane and creates the paradox."

"It may not be as violent as that," said Maitland. "To resolve the paradox, the molecular structure may disintegrate but not the atoms. Or the aircraft may just drop through a 'wormhole' into the alternate universe, where the crystal simply exploded."

"And you're here to see," said Kerowski, admiringly. "It could all have been done by remote, but something crucial might be missed. And you could not delegate the risk to a junior man.

Science does this to us sometimes, does it not?"

Pendleton put a hand on Maitland's shoulder. "If he doesn't get a Nobel Prize out of this, he may get a best-seller to rival *A Brief History of Time*."

"There's a Tornado from Leuchars following the Concorde, as arranged," said Maitland. "The pilot's reported nothing strange, so far."

"Repeat the instruction to keep a distance," said Pendleton. "If we're all wrong about what's going to happen next, we don't want more than one aircraft loss."

Time. One moment the wreckage was on screen; the next, gone. There was an impression that the case containing the crystal had fluoresced. A hundred tons of metal, plastic and thawing flesh disappeared, back to a world which in that moment was launched on to a more different track of history. There was an implosion like a thunderclap as air filled the vacuum; dust swirled up, the walls caved in, the roof came down and the screens went dark. From outside the sound continued as the hangar collapsed.

Pendleton picked up the microphone with a slightly shaky hand. "Zebra One, report on the status of Bravo Oscar Alpha George, over."

Maitland switched on the speaker. "Zebra One to RAE: no change. But I could swear there's something wrong with this visor, or my eyes: for a moment I'm sure I saw two aircraft. Over."

"Roger, Zebra One. Thank you for your assistance. Terminate your observation and return to base, over and out."

And now it was really over. In that other world, Concorde G-BOAG had just disappeared from the radar in Atlantic House, the international air traffic control centre which had replaced Redbrae. There would be a scatter of debris on screen, but there had been no distress call and there would be no alarm, for a moment. "Oscar Alpha George, do you read?" High in *that* Hebridean sky, those people were already dead, killed by the explosion, the decompression or the transonic slipstream. That girl's face was frozen now in that angelic look of calm which had haunted him, here, for so many years, showing that she died with courage. In this building's equivalent, on his desk, in a few minutes the phone would ring.

In this reality, she might be leafing through the in-flight magazine, or accepting champagne now that the airliner had passed the speed of sound. Out over the Atlantic the Concorde was carrying her on to her appointments and contacts in a social world he could never approach, as remote from him as the planet Mars or that other dimension into which her dead body had gone. Her life had crossed with his in real-time for just a few short minutes, when they shared the Heathrow lounge. That it *was* carrying her on, and all the other passengers who had been snatched from death there, would be his only reward.

For these two with him, it might be different. Vast amounts of data had been recorded by Maitland's computers, and he was making sure it had all been copied to the backups in the Atomic Energy Establishment. "It's over to you, now," Pendleton said to Kerowski. "You can tell him what there is to know about that damned rock. Maybe when you get together with his boys, you'll come up with time travel or some similar breakthrough. I'm content with what I've achieved: there's a planeload of people up there, and yourself down here, who would otherwise be dead. Preventing that has been my ambition for all these years. With every accident I've wanted to reach back in time, tell the pilot, stop the baggage handler, somehow prevent it from happening... and just this once, I've been able to do it."

"For the other universe, the consequences are terrible," said the Russian."

"Yes, you're right. Over there the emergency alert has begun, the air-sea rescue organisation is being mobilised. They know where it went off the radar, and eye-witness reports will be coming in. Over there, maybe, another version of me will be packing his bags for a dash to the Hebrides, as I did in 1969. He'll have it all to do—the recovery, the reconstruction—though he'll have all the appropriate information. The flight recorders won't contain any mysteries, and he'll not have to do so much detective work on the people. But he'll be working in the glare of the media, the relatives' grief, recriminations, lawsuits...I'm not sorry to be missing all that."

"You could have saved him all that, and saved their lives in both universes, by not putting the crystal in the wreck!"

"No, you're wrong there. Then it wouldn't have come here, we wouldn't have been forewarned, and the Concorde in this universe would have crashed, and I would have it all to do now. I've done all that could be done, and it can't be taken from me."

"And if I hadn't given you the crystal?"

Pendleton had given serious thought to requisitioning a gun, having no idea what he would face today, but in the end had settled for a pair of handcuffs. He showed them to Kerowski. "If necessary, I'd have chained *you* to the frame. And stood guard by the wreck to the end, in case you got free."

As usual, he avoided the motorway going home, and as usual, pulled into the pub yard at Virginia Water. His ritual pint of real ale had seldom been better deserved. As he nursed it, he kept an eye on the TV above the bar. If his achievement attracted any media attention, it could only be now.

"...In Farnborough and Fleet, Hampshire, today, windows were rattled by a mysterious explosion which caused many calls to emergency services. Later a Ministry of Defence spokesman stated that an obsolete hangar had been demolished in a controlled explosion. No personnel were injured and the Ministry wished to apologise for any inconvenience or alarm which had been caused. Peter Blow has more details."

The picture cut to a helicopter view of the airfield. "Today's demolition at Farnborough was evidently of Hangar T-50 in the Accident Investigation section, made notorious in the 1970's by allegations that the British government used it to conceal a crashed UFO. At Farnborough today, an Air Accident Investigation officer who declined to be named said, as he left the Royal Aerospace Establishment, 'If anything ever was there, I can assure you that it's not there now.'..."

1. Royal Aircraft Establishment (later Royal Aerospace Establishment, now Qinetiq), Farnborough; housing the Accidents Section, then the entire Air Accident Investigation Branch (1980s on) and the National Remote Sensing Centre (1990s).

2. Accident Investigation Branch of the Board of Trade, Shell-Mex House, London; later moved temporarily to Victoria Street, then to Bramshot, Hampshire, finally moved to Farnborough as the Air Accident Branch of Department of Transport (1980s).

3. Royal Air Force station, Benbecula, Outer Hebrides.

4. Royal Artillery Guided Weapons Range, South Uist.

5. Lochboisdale, South Uist.

6. Rocket range tracking station, St. Kilda.

7. U.S. Navy Polaris submarine depot ships, Holy Loch, 1961-1992; Royal Navy nuclear and Polaris submarine bases adjacent.

8. Prestwick International Airport; housed U.S.A.F. Military Air Transport Service and Air Rescue till 1967, later Royal Navy HMS Gannet anti-submarine and air-sea rescue base; also Scottish Aviation Limited (later British Aerospace), and Scottish & Oceanic Air Traffic Control Centre, Redbrae, later moved to Atlantic House, in Prestwick itself.

9. S & OATC radar station, Western Gailes (closed 1979).

10. RAF Lossiemouth (Coastal Command).

11. RAF Macrihanish, Kintyre Peninsula.

12. Royal Aircraft Establishment missile range, Aberporth, Wales.

13. British Aircraft Corporation (later British Aerospace) Concorde production and test facilities, Filton.

14. Liathach Ridge, Glen Torridon, Wester Ross.

15. United Kingdom Atomic Energy Authority, Harwell.

16. Heathrow International Airport; headquarters of British Overseas Aircraft Corporation, later British Airways.

17. RAF Leuchars (Fighter Command).

Notes

On publication of this story in *Analog*, I had a number of letters (e.g. from Bernie Gallagher, of Piscataway, New Jersey) asking if there wasn't more to this story. There is more to be told: the first version was 8,000 words longer and included a lot more of John Pendleton's background, more Air Accident Investigation background, and a sub-plot in which suspicion for the 'hoax' fell (with his permission) on my old friend Archie Roy, Professor of Astronomy at Glasgow University and himself a writer of science-based thrillers. In the map above, Macrihanish and the Liathach Ridge belong in that longer version of the story.

In particular I was asked about The Girl and her body armour, and there's sub-text there which some people miss. If her 'armour' wasn't under development in the 1990s, I'd be surprised. By 1992, AIDS had changed social attitudes a lot. In a rape case shortly before, the defence had argued *unsuccessfully* that the victim had consented, by trying to get her attacker to put on a condom. Five years earlier, it's quite likely that argument would have succeeded. When this story went to press there was still a possibility that heterosexual AIDS would reach epidemic proportions. If it had, there would be a lot of property up for grabs; and those doing the grabbing would be those who were rich and powerful already. Not all of these would be nice people: notice the hint, since she's avoided the news limelight, that the girl may be one of the late John Brunner's 'Totally Rich' (one of the best SF stories ever). There would be power marriages, arranged to consolidate the new groupings of wealth, and for that type of woman, being a virgin on marriage would once again be at a premium. There would be women who were sufficiently ambitious to find a new, comfortable form of chastity belt an acceptable restriction, especially if it also afforded considerable protection against mugging or less casual assault. And it would have its compensations: as long as she added gloves and a hat with a broad brim or a veil, she could sunbathe or swim off southern hemisphere beaches which, if the damage to the ozone layer hadn't been arrested, might well have become almost empty by 1999.

All the places named are real and timescales accurate as far as I know, with two exceptions which are deliberate poetic license. 'Hangar T-50' is imaginary, though numbered consistently with the other Air Accident Investigation Branch buildings at Farnborough; and I moved forward the Conservative victory at the end of the 60s in order to include Edward Heath's amazing *Panorama* confrontation with Robin Day on the question of inflation, where I seem to have been the only UK inhabitant who was listening, rather than denouncing or applauding a mere television interviewer having the gall to press the Prime Minister on an issue of policy.

John Pendleton's career background was that of my friend Peter Alan Blow, a regular (as 'Pablo') in the Irvine and Prestwick Folk Song Clubs in 1966-70. I lost touch with him after that, but it appears his wish to graduate to Air Accident investigation was not fulfilled. Having worked at RAF Benbecula, he made some very helpful comments on my story line, and these were confirmed and added to by Clive Smith of British Aerospace, backup astronaut trainee for the Juno mission to the Mir space station.

On air crash investigation my primary sources were:

E. Colston Shepherd, 'Riddle of the Comet Crash', *New Scientist*, 19th October 1967; V.J. Clancy, 'Comet G-ARCO: Solving the Riddle', *New Scientist*, 12th September 1968.

Fred Jones, "Air Crash, the Clues in the Wreckage", Robert Hale, 1985.

William H. Tench, "Safety Is No Accident", Collins, 1985.

For recommending those last two, and for help on minor points of procedure and background, I have to thank past and present members of the Air Accident Investigation Branch, as it now is. It's sad to have to add (though it's a touch he might have appreciated) that those contacts, making it possible for me to complete the 'land, sea and air' subset of stories, arose indirectly from the untimely death of my cousin's husband, Bill Roberts, late of the National Engineering Laboratory and Rolls-Royce (East Kilbride). British Airways staff were also most helpful, with such details as flight numbers, seating plan and seat allocation. Any remaining errors are entirely my own.

The plane-spotter's complaint about 'G-BOAC' in the airline's artwork was made to me by David Spruell in 1959, as a reason for refusing to buy that year's *BOAC Book of Flight*. As it says in the story, the airline employed it on all its promotional artwork and drove plane-spotters to distraction because they couldn't tell if the picture was of a real aeroplane. When I set out to write 'With Time Comes Concord', I needed a registration number and I looked up a commemorative calendar which British Airways had produced for the Concorde's tenth year in service. I hadn't previously noticed that in the painting on the cover, the registration was G-BOAC—but I stopped laughing when I found the same reg in the photos for January, February and March. Had they been airbrushed? April, however, showed G-BOAF. On investigation, the first Concorde to enter service was designated G-BOAA, which is still known to aviation correspondents as 'Double Alpha'. Then the rest were numbered in sequence, so there really is a G-BOAC, even if we lost it from active service in October 2003. In fact, it was the Concorde used to transport members of the royal family, Prime Ministers etc. on high-prestige trips abroad; and now, it has been relegated to an exhibit at Manchester airport.

I was in a student talents group in 1967 where one of the standing jokes was that to impress people, we would have pocket calculators—each! I was in a bar watching a TV broadcast from Apollo 8, not 10, when an IBM-trained Systems Analyst denounced the whole thing as a hoax because the onboard computer technology was 'impossible'. The scientific calculator in a conference folder discarded in an alleyway, twenty years later, was found by the late Oscar Schwiglhofer, the founder of ASTRA (See notes on 'Riding the Fire'). When digital watches first came out, I was doing well with the line 'But how will you find south with it?', until I tried it on Graeme Duncan of the Hunterston nuclear power station, a keen yachtsman—hence his reply, "Listen, sunshine, if I know what time it is, I know where the bloody Sun is!" The Russian pop stars took longer than I expected, but eventually reached our charts in the attractive forms of TATU.

All the aircraft and missiles mentioned in the text are genuine, but some of the comments may seem surprising. Concorde's history is summarised in the text, but others will be less well known, particularly to American readers.

Airliners

The Vickers Viscount was a very successful 4-engined turbo-prop medium range airliner, flown by British European Airways and many other airlines. The de Havilland Heron was a much smaller piston-engined aircraft, much used by BEA and others in links with the Channel Islands and the Hebrides, for example, including the Air Ambulance service. Herons were used by the armed forces for liaison work and specialised transport operations: they were the mainstay of the Queen's Flight until replaced by the Avro 748.

The de Havilland Comet 1 was the world's first pure-jet airliner, an early success for BOAC until two were lost in 1954 owing to metal fatigue around the cabin windows. Comet 2's and 3's were afterwards used by RAF Transport Command, and the Comet 4 had some success in the 1960s, narrowly beating the Boeing 707 into commercial transatlantic service. However by then it was in direct competition with American 'Big Jets' such as the 707 and the DC-8. A variant of the Comet remained in service with the RAF as the Nimrod until 2010 (see **Coastal**

Defences).

BOAC's subsequent controversial purchases of American airliners were somewhat mitigated by fitting them with British-built engines: much was made of the fact that the 707-420, for example, had Rolls-Royce Conway bypass turbojets. Developing the RB-211 engine with its carbon-fibre compressor blades, for the next generation of wide-bodied jets such as the Tristar, bankrupted Rolls-Royce in its original form. In the story of the apprentice taking unilateral action in the Middle East an earlier make was involved, but even steel turbine blades can take only so much mishandling.

Bombers

The English Electric Canberra held the world altitude record for its class in the early 1950's. It was used operationally in the Suez crisis, and the 'Canberra jet bomber' (Britain's first) was a mainstay of juvenile fiction for most of the decade. It was followed by the development of the three 'V-bombers', the Vickers Valiant, the Handley Page Victor and the Avro Vulcan, which were on 4-minute readiness at Bomber Command airfields throughout Britain during the 1960s. How far they were ahead of their time can be judged from the comment of a USAF officer, watching one of the last Victor tankers come in to land during the Gulf War. Turning to a defence correspondent of the *Daily Telegraph*, he said, "Good God, I didn't know you Brits were into stealth—when does it enter service?"

Valiant bombers were used in the Suez campaign, but too early in their RAF deployment to be effective. The delta-winged Vulcan was used in the raid on Port Stanley airfield early in the Falklands conflict. Ironically, the fuel tanks for this long-range mission were mounted on pylons originally intended for the Blue Steel stand-off bomb (see *Missiles*). This aircraft is now preserved in the air and space museum at East Fortune, near Edinburgh. A Vulcan which was used as a test-bed for the Concorde's Olympus engine crashed and burned during the development programme.

TSR2 was a low-level nuclear strike aircraft with a design

range of 1500 miles, to replace the V-bombers in attacking Soviet targets from the UK. At the time of cancellation in the late '60s, under Labour, it was rumoured that the contour-hugging computer navigation system could not be made sufficiently compact to fit the aircraft. Jewellery made from TSR2 components featured in the BBC's *Tomorrow's World* science programme and at least one fashion programme of the time.

Fighters

During the 1950s under the Conservatives at least 13 supersonic fighters were developed to prototype stage, including the all-rocket Saunders Roe 177. The only one continued was the English Electric P.1, afterwards named the Lightning. It was renowned for its ability to climb vertically for tens of thousands of feet from takeoff, and was used by the RAF's Flying Tigers aerobatic team. That a Lightning could not intercept a Concorde at cruise altitude was one of the telling points in the thesis which gained my late friend John Braithwaite (see notes on 'The Day and the Hour') his degree in Business Administration. There were rumours of Lightnings with rocket propulsion having operated at altitudes of 100,000 feet and in excess of 2000 mph., but I'm assured by experts on the Lightning that they were only rumours.

Transports

The Blackburn Beverley was one of a number of transport aircraft of the '50s, succeeded by the Lockheed C-130 Hercules, components for which were manufactured under license by Scottish Aviation Ltd. at Prestwick.

Coastal Defences

The Avro Shackleton was one of the longest-serving aircraft with the RAF, the last operational squadron being stood down in 1992. Its role in air-sea rescue, anti-submarine operations and fisheries protection was gradually taken over by the Comet-derived Nimrod, now supplanted by the purchase of American AWACS aircraft.

Missiles

Blue Streak was the British Intermediate Range Ballistic Missile, built by Hawker Siddley Dynamics, with technical input from the U.S. Thor programme. The development cost was matched by Australia, in the construction of launch facilities at Woomera. By the late 1950s there were ambitious plans for communications satellites and manned space vehicles; these were blocked by the Conservative government for political reasons and instead Blue Streak became the first stage of Europa, a multinational launcher for scientific satellites. Britain under Labour then withdrew from the Europa project, leaving our European partners with no option but to buy the first stages from us. A series of launches from Woomera and Kourou in French Guyana all failed, although the Blue Streak stage worked perfectly each time. As a gesture of contempt, the European Launcher Development Organisation gave the last one to a Guyanese farmer for use as a chicken coop.

Blue Steel was a stand-off bomb, what today would be called a cruise missile, developed for use with the V-bomber force. Blue Steels were tested with Victors at Woomera in 1962-63. The project was dropped by the Conservatives in favour of purchasing an American air-launched ballistic missile, Skybolt; after this was cancelled, Britain opted for F-111 swing-wing fighters. These failed initially to meet the required performance and reliability, and the orders were cancelled by the Labour government with heavy financial penalties. This caused great resentment, since the swing-wing technology developed by Barnes Wallis had been given away by the Conservatives after the decision not to go ahead with his Swallow supersonic airliner.

In the end, controversially, Britain built its own submarines and warheads for the Lockheed Polaris missile. 'Chevaline' was a top-secret project under Labour to enhance Polaris with multiple warheads—secret because of the Party's outward opposition to nuclear weapons. In 1992 Britain launched a small fleet of huge submarines to carry US Trident missiles with British warheads; at whom they were to be aimed after the Cold War was anybody's guess, but now it's planned to replace them at still greater cost, Russian bombers are once again penetrating British airspace and Russian submarines are reported to be back in British waters.

Sydney Jordan

Riding the Fire

Mikk froze at the controls, waiting for the moment. Now fully opened, the wing over him tugged at the fuselage, striving to rise. In this gusting wind from the sea, he had to catch the lift at the right point to take him up and away from the rock.

Now! He slapped the release knob and the catapult hurled him forward. He was off the rail, he was airborne, soaring in the updraught, moving the stick right and left as the wing tried to roll to port, a nasty little trick which all pilots of the Lucifer plane knew to allow for. His timing had been almost perfect; the wind whistled in the creaking struts behind him, the buzz of the stall-warning tab on the trailing edge reassured him that he had plenty of flying speed. Safely clear of the slope, he turned and let the wind bring him round in a long swoop, waving a gloved hand to the launch crew before he brought back the stick and began the diagonal ascent of the cone. Four traverses of the upwind face, and then he was over the summit, searching across it for the thermal from the lava lake. The volcano was quiet today, morning mist clinging to the inner slopes of the crater, reddened where it reflected the fires below.

The solid-state radar altimeter resumed the comforting beeps, rising in pitch, which told him he was gaining height. Round and around he went, the summit crags dropping away, the outer slopes again in view, then the surrounding badlands so laboriously crossed yesterday. Now he could see the fields of the settlement, and beyond them the sea, but incoming clouds were beginning to spoil the view. The beeping flattened out and he tacked to rediscover the wavering column of warm air. In the distance, now, on the horizon, was the dark mass and plume of Aetna, the next staging point in his journey.

Lucifer was a planet dotted with volcanoes, larger and younger than Earth, its core and crust impregnated with the radioactive elements which stoked its fires. On an early photograph from orbit, with the volcanoes tagged in red at the end of each smoke plume, some pilot had written 'like an oil-field in the Gulf'—a reference to an old war, and not one of the great ones, but visually apt: Earth hadn't shown a landscape as *geologically* active since long before there were geologists to study it.

In one respect Lucifer was ideal for colonisation: the land masses were barren, though the seas teemed with life and the atmosphere was breathable. Integrating terrestrial life into the biosphere of an earthlike, life-supporting world was a task no biologist would normally attempt—not when there were sterile but otherwise earthlike worlds which could be terraformed so much more easily. Lucifer was a borderline case because the continents were lifeless: the plants and the bottom-crawlers had no way to leave the tidal pools when it was certain, on evolutionary timescales, that any adaptations would vanish under a fresh blanket of lava.

So life had made no inroads from the coast until humans arrived—dispossessed, homeless or impoverished humans who would risk staking out a planet which might not be significant in the galactic trade wars for centuries, if ever. Out there among the stars, where huge corporations traded in whole solar systems, someone had thought this world might be strategically useful. It could be colonised with a small investment of resources—much less than for a terraforming project—by people sufficiently desperate to grab the few patches of stable terrain, able to house a hundred to a thousand at most, and willing to terraform those patches or die in the attempt. Willing to learn to fly and to land, not in big safe capsules, but in one and two-person winged planes which would be the robust basis of inter-settlement links for generations—even if those generations had no other technology, and even if they lost tens of planes per year. With 5000 landers, mass-produced by a von Neumann machine on some carbonaceous asteroid, the Lucifer fleet would take a long time to run out.

Thus the Lucifer plane: a one or at most a two-person carrier, built entirely of carbon fibre; the fuselage solid, the wing a woven mesh braced by spars which radiated fanwise from the nose and by two massive, hinged struts from the mid-fuselage to the leading edge. For atmosphere entry, with the fuselage uppermost, it was a double-cavity Waverider: hit lower air, vary the geometry of the leading edge, half-roll, rotate the cockpit 180 degrees, and you had a hang-glider. All you had to do after that was get down, on an unfamiliar planet bigger than Earth, at one of the few sites where life was possible, where the kamikaze scouts were waiting.

Not all had made it. Some pulled excessive g's on entry, disintegrated the fibre structure and died high in the atmosphere. Some made the roll too violent, lost one or both wings, and fell like broken birds or like bullets. And some, inevitably, went astray and landed on the jagged lava, far from hope of rescue.

Most of them made it, nevertheless. Of necessity, more than half of them were pilots, and there were planes for all who were. But in the next generation, not all had the aptitude, and in any case most were wholly occupied in trying to farm, to maintain basic skills and the background knowledge which would allow the colony to build up, once it became obvious that no more help was coming from outside. Whatever the trading gambit had been, apparently it didn't come off, and for the foreseeable future, Lucifer was on its own. With the focus on survival, nobody dragged gliders across the lava and up the sides of the mountains to launch unless it was necessary. After two generations, already pilots were a select and privileged few—a few whom Mikk had always wanted to join and whose privileges he had always wanted to share. In his dreams he had saved many a settlement, single-handed.

If he had been in the first generation, of course, his approach would have been perfect. Nobody had flown an atmosphere entry for five generations, since the colonists were dropped here and left to fend for themselves; but in his dreams and daydreams Mikk had done it often, riding the fire down towards where the sky was familiar, the plumes of the volcanic peaks rising out of the landscape to become level with his wings, and it all rolling over him, then back, as the conversion was made. He had lived through that one, vicariously, as often as he had flown Camels or Spitfires, Phantoms or F-16's. In his mind he always flew the best, and he was the hottest pilot of them all.

Yesterday, in the control tower on the rain-swept settlement landing field, the Briefing Officer had seen his abilities rather differently. "This flight's an ascending staircase—you shouldn't be flying it. Nobody should, with less than a thousand solo hours. *You're* supposed to be on a milk run round the coast, picking up and dropping mail just to get some experience."

This man was out of the air before his time, smashed up on a lava outcrop just short of some landing field, and he had no time for would-be bold young pilots. But he had no-one else to send. The New Andes were erupting, inland, and had breached one of the natural nuclear reactors of Lucifer's crust—what geologists called 'the Oklo effect'. Radioactive ash was falling on New Quito, and iodine from the coast was needed urgently. "Stick to your training, stick to the flight plan. No short cuts, no heroics, no fancy flying. People are depending on us, children especially—it's not a job for you but you're all there is."

And after that, the first fishing crew back into harbour were detailed to get him and his plane across the lava field, up the side of Vesuvius, and safely into the air. He had often imagined himself flying a mercy mission like this, succeeding by daring and skill against impossible odds. Unfortunately, the weather was perfect for cross-country flying and although the route was demanding, the odds were entirely in his favour. This wouldn't get him into the inner circle of fire-riders, not unless something went badly wrong and yet he survived it; but it would show them something he knew, with all the confidence of nineteen Earth years—that he was good enough to be one of the best of them.

Unexpectedly, on the long glide towards Aetna, Mikk heard the muted tone of the beeper change. At once he turned up the volume and circled, seeking out the unmapped thermal with the infrared sight embedded in his windscreen. It wasn't a strong one and lifted him only a few hundred feet, but it was important. It might mark a new volcanic hot-spot, and if so the geologists would be interested: every change on the dynamic crust of this plant told them something new. Geological monitoring was constant, in a situation where one peak could block the way to a dozen settlements when it was active. No-one was crazy enough to fly into that kind of violence. The air within an erupting plume was no hotter than re-entry, and in theory the aircraft could stand it, but it was filled with turbulence, lightning and red-hot flying rocks.

More immediately important was that the rising air might save a life some day—perhaps his own. If you ran out of lift and had to set down on those waterless badlands, virtually impassible on foot, there was nowhere for rescuers to land by you or to take off again. There had been a few epics—pilots sustained by air-drops of food and water while they walked out—but to get the supplies within reach on a lava field, by a technique first used in the jungles of Earth, you needed a long, long rope, plenty of height and plenty of lift. Until the colony re-attained powered flight, retrieving downed aircraft and pilots was generally impossible.

Across the land-mass of Lucifer, the glider paths were now well-known. In the early, learning days, enough pilots had been carried off course by unexpected winds to find the ways back if there were any. Each had its surprises, its bonuses and its hidden traps. Most talked about were the staircases: the milk-runs where each volcano in sequence was lower than the last, and the much harder paths where you had to gain more height each time. Mikk was flying one of those, and that was why he had taken off in early morning, so that the ground below would grow hotter as the day wore on.

Aetna was before him now, and with the extra lift he had gained, the approach was no problem. The pilots had all had the experience of running out of lift over the plains: diving suicidally towards the slopes of the next volcano, catching the updraught that took you up over the rim, nosing in over the smoking ramparts, and that desperate wing-tip turn that put you either in the rising column, or corkscrewing down into the lava lake. There was no need to remind yourself not to breathe, the survivors said: you had to remind yourself to start breathing again when you were out of it, circling up and clear.

Of those who had failed to find the updraught on the outside, there were a very few who had made the plunging turn off the slope, survived the turbulence at the volcano's base, and landed within walking distance of some settlement. There were very few volcanoes near settlements, though out of necessity all the settlements were near volcanoes. For any other location, it was better to go straight in and end it quickly.

His next staging point was Arsia—higher than Aetna, but named for the great volcano on Mars because it had a similar huge rift in its side, where the cone had crumpled between parallel faults and provided an escape route for the lava lake to pour out and solidify on the plains below. Sailing in along it was like being an insect inside one of Earth's ancient burial chambers—and there was always the risk of more rockfalls from the overhanging crags. But the true risk was inside the cone, dangerously low over the lava lake, where the air was unbreathable and the turbulence could be extreme. The payoff was the virtual certainty of finding strong lift as soon as you entered the crater—enough to take you swiftly back to breathable air and high enough to fly safely on. Pilots who had flown so low called it 'sharing the dragon's breath'.

Of those who had literally shared the volcano's breath, taking an involuntary searing gasp low within the caldera, there were no survivors at all. Nevertheless, the impulse to ride the fire was built into all of them. Mikk's instructor, Johan, had done it on a training flight when he could as easily have turned away. Mikk had survived it, taking no breath inside the fiery zone—indeed, he had thought he would never breathe again. He was a probationary member of the fire-riders, in them but not of them, not until he flew the manoeuvre with control in his hands. When that moment came, there would be no witnesses; but he would know it had happened, and the change it would work in him would be obvious to the rest.

Mid-afternoon found him still climbing the staircase, but with only one range still to cross. Ahead lay Kilimanjaro, named for its African counterpart because it was high enough to catch and freeze moisture from its own outgassing and from the upper airstreams crossing the continent. In the centuries since the last major eruption, the cone had become encased in gleaming ice and the build-up stayed ahead of the rock-dust and sulphur coming out of the crater. The run-off from its glaciers was beginning to form fans of soil on the plains, potential sites for future settlements.

Though the incoming weather from the sea had seemed threatening when he took off, he had stayed far before it and the sun had baked the badlands all day, with the steady increase in general lift he had hoped for. In the last hundred kilometres he had lost virtually no height, the following wind helping to keep up his groundspeed, and he had little soaring to do to breast the summit of the volcano. As he crossed the snow-fields of the wide rim, light strained through the mesh of his wings made his enlarged shadow look like the wide-cast net of some giant fisher.

The image was all too appropriate, because Kilimanjaro had set a trap for him. Though it hadn't been obvious from the outside, and there had been no warning from the geologists, the great caldera was active, its lava higher than ever seen before and boiling, glimpsed through roiling clouds of flame. The central updraught was correspondingly more powerful and the surrounding downdraught correspondingly fierce—in a crater of this size, he had no chance to get across in these conditions. The descending airstream caught him and pulled him down, forcing him to turn away from where safety lay as the stall-warning tab went ominously quiet. He had to turn towards the rocks, angle his wings parallel to the inner slope of the cone, and go whirling down—gaining speed all the way, till the rocks were only a blur, but without gathering enough momentum to be able to beat centrifugal force and get to the centre of the deadly funnel.

The rate-of-descent beeps had merged into a scream, and he might have joined it if breathing wasn't bound to be fatal. He was down in the fire-mist and immersion in the lava could only be seconds away. The worst of it might be that the carbon-fibre hull would withstand the heat—for a time. Preferable, perhaps, if he could find the nerve, to crack the canopy before the impact and let the molten rock engulf him. But to let go the stick now would be to admit there was no chance, however small, that an eddy would whirl him into the rising thermal. And now it was too late...

Much too late! The lava lake had vanished and he was in thick smoke, shot through with sparks, penetrating his cockpit and driving out the sulphurous fumes of the volcano. There was still fire below but it was true fire, buildings wrapped in flames. Even as the updraught from them expanded his wings, an explosion from below thrust him upwards, fighting again for control. Below, as far as he could see, there were buildings on fire.

The idea that he might be dead flashed through his mind, and was as instantly dismissed. He was still at the controls of the Lucifer plane, with all its familiar sensations—still alive, gasping for breath, sweat blurring his vision as the turbulence from below buffeted his wings. What mattered was to gain height, remain in control...the rising beeps of the altimeter and the buzz of the warning tab were more comforting than ever before.

Other sounds were more disturbing, but as his confusion and panic began to subside, he began to make sense of them—incredible though they seemed. He had *gone* somewhere, in that moment of discontinuity before his reflexes kicked in to keep the plane in the air. Yet there was no settlement of this size on Lucifer, not anywhere. What was below him had to be a city—and furthermore, a city under attack, from the air. The whistles and the painful explosions had to be falling bombs; the very different hammering had to be the guns of the defenders. Beams of light stabbed up through the smoke, sweeping the sky and sometimes catching the silver shape of an aircraft before it jinked away. All around him the conflict raged, conflict which was clearly one-sided. As he gained time to think, the outrage of what was happening began to sink in, mixing with a nausea which wasn't all due to the sickly reek of the smoke.

Turning around to stay in the thermals, Mikk tacked over the city like a bird of ill-omen. The Lucifer plane's black, nonreflecting mesh was unlikely to be seen from the ground, and wouldn't show on radar if they had it. Even if he was briefly caught by a searchlight crew they'd be unlikely to differentiate him from the blackness of the sky: they were looking for birds of prey, much higher up. A greater hazard, revealed dully by the fires and in brief stroboscopic flashes by the bombs, was that there were some tall buildings in the smoke—some at least only burned-out shells, without even the reflections of the flames in their windows to warn him on approach.

Eventually the whole city must be reduced to that state, and with nothing left to burn down there, he must run out of lift and have to come down. His chances as an airman among survivors might be little better than on the barren plains at home. It was amazing that he could even think of that, while the bombardment continued without mercy. What had happened to him? Where was home, and where was this? Surely it could only be Earth, but if so, *when* was this? There had been no war like this for many centuries before humans reached out to the stars.

Overhead, the lights and the guns had found a victim. The twists of the bomber as it tried to escape seemed to be in slow-motion: diverging cones of light and converging ones of tracers held it fast. The tracers became an upward blizzard as more batteries shifted target. Flames blossomed from an engine and abruptly the aircraft flipped over, twisting in the remorseless light beams as it spiralled earthwards. A parachute streamed away and opened, startlingly white against the blackness of the sky, and at last the gunners were convinced and turned to seek another attacker.

Though out of the lights, the plunging bomber was still marked by the fire behind it. Mikk side-slipped towards it, hoping to glimpse a marking or recognise a shape that would tell him where he was. As it passed him, sure enough, he recognised the silhouette—and the Iron Crosses on the wings...It was too much, it pushed him finally into disbelief. This had to be illusion, *had* to be, even if it wasn't consistent and he was still in the Lucifer plane, not up there in a Beaufighter making more kills than Cunningham...

Trying to see, he had got too close to the Heinkel. Its slipstream caught him and down he went, fighting again for control. The glider was on its back and in a moment of inspiration he hit the switches that hadn't been used for a century, converting the wing to its rigid Waverider mode. It was just in time: a moment later the bomber crashed directly below him, bomb-load and fuel going up in one huge flash. The blast caught him and threw him upwards, up, up and still up. Darkness, fire and noise vanished together and he was back over Kilimanjaro—*high* over it, safely in the thermal, the last lungful of smoke-filled air expelled violently to prevent an embolism even as he rolled the plane back over to normal flight.

Though he had been in the battle for little more than an hour it was now early evening, the clouds over the volcanoes becoming red in the dusk, a corner of moon gleaming on a dark edge higher up. The New Andes lay ahead, several of the peaks thrusting out plumes of dust which towered far past his height and glowed fiercely in their lower regions, while the rivers of lava on their flanks stood out brightly in the gathering dark. Somehow he kept flying, though he lost all count of time, still battling in his mind with the extraordinary vividness of the hallucination. He must have found the updraught at the last moment, when he had already shared the dragon's breath, and all the time that his mind was possessed, he must have been climbing slowly within it. This must be the secret of the fire-riders, something you had to experience before you could credit it: something so powerful that it brought your knowledge to life, took you back into the early history of aviation.

Before he knew it he was at his destination, still with enough height over the cooling landscape to get down safely on the settlement plateau, between the luminescent markers of the runway. It wasn't a good landing, the nose slamming down hard as soon as the tail-skid made contact, but the ground crew were quickly round him to raise the canopy and help him clear. Now the reaction hit him, a belated fit of coughing to rid his lungs of soot and a fit of the shakes which made him unable to help in the folding of the carbon-mesh wings. Unable even to speak, he disengaged himself from the operation and walked towards the Dispersal, fighting his trembling all the way.

New Quito must have called for a wide range of supplies, because there were an unusual number of aircraft ahead; parked, wings folded, like prehistoric winged reptiles or the first toothed birds. Normally, if a pilot came in so late, there would be a line of pilots waiting to greet him, to brush the Debriefing Officer aside with good humour and force him to get his report on a beer-soaked table in the bar. But there was only one figure waiting for him, half-illuminated by the bright windows of the pilots' Mess.

As Mikk approached, he saw that it was Johan. It seemed appropriate—if he could tell anyone, it would be this man—but he could think of nothing to say.

"It's happened to you, then," said Johan. "You've been to the city."

"What? How could you know?"

"We get a feeling," said Johan. "A lot of the fellows are here, you'll notice...But the smell tells us for sure. The aircraft comes back with the stink of burning homes—if ever you've experienced it, the smell of a burned-out house is never forgotten. It'll take you days to get rid of it; the ground crew radioed in about it before they even got you out."

"But—but—with all the smells we come back with, how could

they know to watch for that one?"

"Because there's an ex-pilot in every ground crew, and it's happened to all of us. It *keeps* happening."

"All of it? The city, the bombs, the flames? The lights, the guns? Are you saying it *really* happened?"

"There's plenty of evidence that it's real. Planes have come back with bullet-holes, sometimes with shrapnel in them...and with thorough debriefing, we can usually identify the city. If there were bombs falling continuously, it probably was London, Tokyo or Dresden. If it's just a sea of fire, it's Hiroshima. One spire is Coventry, two spires and a river is Cologne, and so on."

"But..." It had been hard to believe at the time, impossible to believe afterwards, but this produced another split reaction. It was reassuring to know that he wasn't insane, but staggering to find his experience was commonplace. "It's happened to you—to all of you? Why don't you tell us?"

"Well, would you? Especially if you were the first? Even if you *thought* you were the first—it happened a lot of times before anyone recognised the smell on someone else's aircraft. Then it turned out many of the pilots had been through it. Since it already was a secret, it seemed best to keep it that way."

"Why?" He would have believed almost anything his heroes told him, but it was hard to believe that they'd keep something like this quiet—even if it did explain why sharing the dragon's breath changed people so much. "What *is* the secret? Why does it happen? *How* does it happen?"

"As to why: obviously, it's directed; purposive, not just a force of nature. To keep us in the air, there has to be lift, and whatever sends us back makes sure there's plenty of it. At first, pilots thought that was all there was to it—something knew they were in trouble and got them out. But it's always a city in flames—never a forest fire, for instance. It's almost always under attack from the air, so it's almost always the Second World War. And of course, because people who want to be pilots are usually crazy about old battles, we realise where we are. It's not just to save our lives, there's much more point to it than that."

"If we could choose how to go back, we'd be rocket pilots, or fighter aces..."

"Even when it was happening, there were a few pilots who saw war in the air from both sides, and wrote about it. When one was on the ground, recovering after being shot down, he was caught in an air-raid and a woman who recognised his uniform cried to him, "Why aren't you up there too?" At first he was angry, protesting that he was on her side, and then he realised that there was a sense in which the war was between airmen and civilians, whatever their nationality.

"Now, we have the start of a civilisation on Lucifer which depends on airmen for its links, and someone, something, is telling us that the behaviour of the past won't be permitted. Is it significant, do you think, that the planet and the planes are both called Lucifer? The corresponding Greek name was Phosphorus, which is also a chemical used in incendiary bombs. In medieval times Lucifer came to be a name for the Devil, but originally it was the Roman name for Venus as the morning star, the bringer of light and hope—as we're supposed to be for the settlers. The bombers are our antithesis, but we have to see it to know it."

"But who's making it happen?"

"Well, the time-gates are volcanoes. We go back to real cities, identifiable in debrief, but there's not always war. If you go back a second time it's Pompeii, or Santorini, or Mont Pelée, as if to show us what volcanoes themselves can do. We've wondered if they're warning us to leave the planet, or saying they approve of burning cities, but that's not it."

"You don't mean—!" Running out of belief, Mikk ran out of words. Was he being told that his heroes were part of a cult, worshipping gods under the volcanoes—like something out of the cultural sections of his training, the ones he had skipped whenever the teaching machines allowed?

"It's possible." Johan waved an arm at the row of parked Lucifers, to which Mikk's had now been added. "The earliest aircraft were wood and fabric, ready to burn at the smallest spark. Could their makers have imagined a cloth which could withstand atmosphere entry and the heat of a volcano? We can't imagine life which could exist under the crust of a planet, and it'll be a long time before we have the scientific resources to investigate. Certainly it couldn't be life as we know it, but there's sentience here *somewhere*. With the power to send us back down the time-line of our own history, make us face the things we've done that we'd rather forget. We're being told they won't stand for that here. So any time you find yourself getting too cocky, too full of your worth as a pilot, especially thinking how good you'd be at war in the air—just stop and ask: who does this planet *really* belong to?"

Involuntarily, they both looked at the glowing summits surrounding them in the night, before turning away to the Mess and the welcome of their fellow pilots.

Notes

This story, which added 'fire' to 'land, sea and air' to complete 'The Elements of Time', was provisionally accepted by Amazing Stories, subject to some minor changes which weren't made in time before the magazine ceased publication. Much of the inspiration came from Terence Nonweiler, formerly Professor of Aeronautics at Glasgow University and an Honorary Member of ASTRA, the Association in Scotland to Research into Astronautics. In 1967 he took part in discussions which led to my book "Man and the Stars".[1] For landing on an Earthlike world, he strongly advocated winged space vehicles, and for landing in unknown terrain, he insisted on 'time to enquire' over the landing site. In this and in later meetings which led to "New Worlds for Old"[2] and "Man and the Planets"[3], he dismissed arguments that more sophisticated systems than wings would in time become available: wherever you have a planet with an atmosphere, a wing, which makes use of the properties of that atmosphere, is more elegant than something which wastes energy staying aloft by other means.

Nonweiler was the inventor of the Waverider re-entry vehicle, intended to be the manned spacecraft in a British space programme based on the Blue Streak missile. The programme was cancelled by the Macmillan government, but work on Waverider continued for a time at the Royal Aircraft

Establishment, to assess Waverider's potential as a Mach 6 airliner. Thereafter Waverider was largely forgotten, except by enthusiasts such as ASTRA, but after years of campaigning it's back on the international scientific map. In October 1990 the University of Maryland hosted the First International Hypersonic Waverider Conference, co-sponsored by NASA, and the delegates present numbered nearly a hundred.

The Waverider wing is folded downwards. Travelling at several times the speed of sound, it generates a plane shockwave below it, attached to the leading edges; consequently the shape of the under-wing cavity has to be related to the planform (the shape of the vehicle, seen from above). A delta planform gives the shape which is known as the 'caret wing', because from the rear it looks like an inverted 'V' or a printer's caret. A Concorde-type planform gives a cavity shaped like a Gothic arch; this was the one which the Royal Aircraft Establishment evolved as best for their Mach 6 airliner design. Its low wing-loading gives it a landing 'footprint', descending from space, which literally envelops the Earth, and a touchdown speed of less than 160 kph. When it comes to developing the Solar System's resources a delivery vehicle which can land anywhere on Earth, on ordinary runways, will be of great political importance.

The US Air Force and the University of Maryland developed an alternative version of Waverider, which has removed most of its original characteristics except for the high-speed manoeuvrability. It was flown as the nosecone of the X-51, an experimental prototype of a Mach 6 cruise missile, intended to hit targets up to 60 miles away without risk to aircrew in the B-52 carrier. In November 2010 *Time Magazine* hailed Waverider as no. 4 in the fifty best inventions of 2010.[4] Terence Nonweiler would have hated what's happened to his invention, and as a pacifist he would have hated what the X-51 concept stands for. In his 1970 lecture to ASTRA he had attributed the lack of interest in Waverider to its lack of military applications, and considered it a small price to pay. If we can, we shall reclaim the territory for Nonweiler's version of the Waverider and its peaceful applications.

In 1992 Gordon Dick (who has since changed his name to

Gordon Ross) and I drafted an article, 'Flight in Non-Terrestrial Atmospheres', including a Waverider carrier for a Venus surface explorer, a flexible aircraft for Mars exploration, and a Waverider factory for the atmosphere of Jupiter.[5] *Analog* editor Stanley Schmidt asked us also to consider worlds which would be like Earth, yet sufficiently different to need different designs. Following an earlier suggestion by L.H. Townend,[6] Gordon came up with two flexible Waverider shapes, the Lucifer Plane and the Altair, allying his previous experience in sails and hang-glider design to Nonweiler's theory.

The conditions allowing human occupation of planets were examined by Stephen H. Dole in the fascinating book "Habitable Planets for Man"[7] the allowable range was from 0.04 of Earth's mass to 2.35, to retain a breathable atmosphere at one end and to keep surface gravity below 1.5g at the other. The lower limit of atmospheric pressure is set by mountaineering experience, the upper by deep-sea diving, with partial pressures of oxygen and other gases adjusted accordingly. The temperature range has to permit water to exist as solid, liquid and gas... When we look at the effect this has on aircraft design, the answer is that if something will fly on Earth, it'll fly on any other Earthlike world, with more or less payload depending on the exact set of conditions.

Considering the extremes, we came up independently with a world younger than Earth, perhaps larger (though not too large), with more radioactive material in its crust, and lots of volcanic activity. With all that thermal lift around, the occupants could use hang-gliders for transport—and they'd probably need them, because settlements would be separated by impassable badlands. An atmosphere entry vehicle should also be able to withstand temperatures inside the crater of a volcano; but could it be lightweight *and* robust enough to do both?

Gordon Dick's Lucifer plane is built almost entirely of carbon fibre, and its wings are a carbon-fibre mesh which will let enough plasma through to survive the heat of entry. Mesh parachutes for braking during atmosphere entry have been under study since the early 1950's. For a ballistic vehicle they increase the landing 'footprint'; you might think that for a

Waverider they contract it, since the lift of the wing is reduced, but as drag is also reduced the crucial lift/drag ratio is little altered. The wing is braced by struts radiating fanwise from the nose and by two hinged spars from the fuselage to the leading edges. On the way into atmosphere, the fuselage is uppermost and the wing is a double-cavity Waverider. Liquid hydrogen bled through the struts carries away heat at the trailing edges, possibly for ignition on an external burning surface to provide thrust. Once down into the troposphere, in a manoeuvre which will require careful timing and judgement, the pilot rolls it on to its back, adjusts the geometry of the leading edge by varying the spread of the fan, and rotates the cockpit 180 degrees so that he or she is no longer upside-down. With that, the plane is in hang-glider mode—probably for the rest of its operational life, unless the colony has the capability to put it back into space as a mini-shuttle.

The tail assembly also rotates, out of the way for landing; and of course the wing can be folded, for compact parking. For unless we assume that this imaginary colony has the capability from the outset to keep *powered* aircraft flying, then the Lucifer planes will continue to be gliders as they maintain transport links between settlements. So they'll need to be small and light enough to be dragged up the volcanoes for re-launch; so thousands of them will be needed to take down the population of a viable terrestrial colony; so they'll be mass-produced, probably by a von Neumann machine on some carbonaceous asteroid... and the Lucifer settlements will have enough of them to maintain contact, even if it takes centuries to build up local industries and conditions are so bad that tens of planes are lost every year meantime.

Versions of this design could live in almost any imaginable atmosphere, Earthlike or not; But one world will be off-limits to Lucifer planes: Venus, whose sulphuric acid smog would turn their carbon-fibre structure into candyfloss with terrifying speed—not to mention the low surface winds, and the need for armour. And Venus is described in most textbooks as a terrestrial planet, on size and mass. So to make an all-Terran as well as all-terrain version, which the article went on to discuss, we must either produce a material which will let the plane go to Venus, yet still fly in all those other atmospheres; or we can just make Venus and any sister worlds habitable, so making their atmospheres 'terrestrial' in the sense which our article began with.

References

1. Duncan Lunan, "Man and the Stars", Souvenir Press, 1974; US edition "Interstellar Contact", Henry Regnery Co., 1975.

2. Duncan Lunan, "New Worlds for Old", David & Charles, 1979; US edition William Morrow Inc..

3. Duncan Lunan, "Man and the Planets", Ashgrove Press, 1983.

4. Richard Corliss et al, 'The 50 Best Inventions of 2010', *Time*, 176, 21, 48 (November 22nd, 2010).

5. Duncan Lunan and Gordon Dick, 'Flight in Non-Terrestrial Atmospheres, or the Hang-glider's Guide to the Galaxy', *Asgard* 2, 4, ASTRA, April 1992; shorter version *Analog Science Fiction/ Science Fact*, January 1993.

6. L.H. Townend, "The Waverider", APECS Limited, 1983.

7. Stephen H. Dole, "Habitable Planets for Man", Blaisdell Publishing Company, 1964.

Verdict of History

"**Y**ou are brought before us** on the charge of witchcraft. How do you plead?"

The building in which the trials took place was an all-wooden structure. Walls, floor, roof and beams, benches, table, judges' chairs, lectern and gavel, all were of local wood, roughly finished but the solid, reliable work of local men. Even the engines of torture in the next room had scarcely a metal nail in their construction; they took a pride in their work, the joiners and carpenters of this town. Only the shackles on the man accused were of iron—and his bearing, voice and manner were pure steel.

"I plead for nothing from you. There is nothing which I want from you and nothing which you have to give!"

"You have God's mercy and forgiveness to seek—" said the priest "—and we have justice and retribution to give out," the chief judge added, so promptly that it must have been said before. They knew their business, these men: they too were thorough in their work. "State your name, and say now plainly: are you innocent or guilty?"

"My name is Mohan," said the stranger. "It is just a name, it signifies nothing. I have travelled far and experienced many things; I am guilty of all things and innocent of everything. In this time and place I am guilty of nothing: I have had dealings with no-one and committed no acts. Why have you set upon me and brought me here?" His anger made the onlookers uneasy. Such energy and fearlessness were far out of the ordinary for the accused at such a trial, yet he did not seem evil or possessed. He was in control of all his faculties; his sheer confidence made it seem as if the judges themselves were on trial.

"The evidence against you is straightforward, however extraordinary your name," said the Inquisitor, "and we shall learn soon enough what *that* may signify. You were arrested in the public street, enquiring for a young woman who was tried here and burned a week since for the good of her soul and the health of the community. Her guilt was utterly beyond doubt. Yours, as an associate of hers, appears to be beyond question. Let us have no more evasions—answer the questions of the court!"

"Tell me more, then. I came here to search for a young woman, and you tell me she is dead. By whom was she accused, and on what evidence was she convicted?"

"She was accused by all. Her beauty was unnatural, her language and manners extraordinary. Put to the question, she appeared impervious to pain. On the ducking-stool, she seemed able to breathe under water, and the water itself seemed to reject contact with her. Under duress, and all the way to the stake, she never once called upon God or His saints for mercy, but always to unseen personages and powers for assistance—assistance which was denied to her only because we are God-fearing people, protected by Heaven and our own watchfulness. Try to escape as she did, call uselessly upon demons for aid!"

"There are no demons," said the prisoner, "no, nor any God such as you worship."

"Silence him!" cried the judges, and the guards sprang forward, but somehow he eluded their grasp. "Suffer little children to come unto me, said Christ—it was never God's chosen who put children to the fire in their worship!" The guards struck at him with their staves to stop the blasphemy, but still somehow they failed to connect. The anger of the accused man knew no bounds. "I proclaim your church profaned, and your town accursed, by the terrible things which these men have done—and I mark them now with a sign as to whom they truly serve!"

All that could be said afterwards by the witnesses (who would have said more if they could) was that he moved then to a place where the shackles happened not to be. Deprived of his support, they fell to the floor with a clang. At the same moment, there appeared in his hands a weapon which resembled a pistol, though much smaller, and having in place of a barrel a simple rod of glass. From it came an intense beam of light which generated smells of burning and other odours of the Pit. Mohan did not aim for the eyes of his accusers, but swept the beam across their faces with a stroke which raised livid brands on each. As they leaped up or fell back with screams of pain, chaos broke out in the crowded room. Many of those present were later to swear that they had tried to apprehend him, indeed to swear most bitterly as to the efforts they had made. But he passed unseen through the midst of them, like—it was whispered afterwards—like Christ on the brow of the hill at Nazareth; and went his way. But the whispers were very quiet; and when the trials began again, a scant five days later, very soon they were silenced altogether.

The second courtroom was all of metal—floor, walls and ceiling; a window-less box. If windows were needed the computers could provide them, with the necessary views, just as they now provided the ancient flag and the emblems of justice. The metal of the room was not of Earth at all, having come from a rock so far from the Sun that the Earth could scarcely be glimpsed from it, and the room itself may not have been on Earth—where it was, and how big it was (a foot on a side or a thousand miles) were of no consequence. All human business was conducted within such boxes when the psychological factors called for the provision of a 'room'. where the boxes were, how big they were, what they were made of or where it came from, were matters of no consequence to those who used them. Everything in them which mattered was projected—optically, if the participant wore a mechanical or organic body, but otherwise directly into the mind. Mohan's awareness was concentrated within an organic but artificial body which (mediaeval impurities apart) closely resembled the one he had occupied at the previous trial. The judges' projections took the forms of their fancy, within the part of their Higher-order awareness which they were devoting to the trial—an adequate part to let Mohan be tried by his peers, in a sense, according to ancient convention.

"The charge against you is Intervention. What have you to reply?"

Everything in the room was of metal, but Mohan's stance, manner and delivery were wooden. "For the record—what is your evidence?"

"For the record—you were in link with the Net throughout your mission. From the time when you learned that target recovery was impossible, you acted without regard to the constraints of the epoch. You set yourself in judgment upon the time and the people of the time—you said as much openly and you allowed them to see that you had a differing viewpoint and perspective. You displayed abilities which in that time could only be perceived as supernatural, and you called upon weaponry from far outside its technological horizon."

"In pre-Net fiction," said Mohan, "there was a cliché for all of this. I broke the Prime Directive. Is that the charge?"

"Neither the action nor the charge is a cliché," said the voice from the bench. "Since you risk expulsion from the Net, I counsel you against a defence based on pre-Net values—whether you spoke for them or against them, they would be too simplistic to affect the balance of your case."

"To Hell with the balance of the case! Not to intervene, or to reveal oneself within a less advanced culture, was the 'Prime

Directive' of pre-Net fiction—rules laid down for travel in space and time by people who were capable of neither! Now we operate as a species in mind-machine link, on levels so sophisticated that most of us never penetrate into them. Yet we can penetrate the pre-Net past of the species, to observe, to study—but never to intervene!"

"When mind-machine links were achieved, all of humanity was drawn in by their lure," said the voice—not even from the judges, Mohan suspected, but from the computers through whom they 'spoke'. "If we are not to stagnate as a species, the Net must have a continuous influx of fresh, original views. As they reach adolescence and become aware of the Net, and before they are seduced by its full potential, the young must come to understand what the pre-Net past of humanity truly was."

"The child you sent me to retrieve learned that in full," Mohan replied, his anger at the mediaeval trial rekindled. "A teenager, slipping away from her study group, with no more skills than to block mild pain and to keep the rain off—unable to move in time without the help of a guardian—not even knowing how to call through time to the Net—and put to death in terror and agony! The price is too great. What if we do intervene—what of it? You may call my reaction immature—you can invoke the supreme penalty and remove me from the Net—but I've proved it can be done. I've changed history, whatever happens—I've stopped those monstrous trials in their tracks!"

As the voice of the court replied, the images of the judges darkened and the emblems of justice faded. "It has all been tried before: it was stopped only because we risked losing all sight of our true origins. The trials which you thought to stop resumed again within the week, more ferociously than before, and lasted for longer. Computations of the causative effect of your actions suggest that artists, composers and statesmen were lost in succeeding centuries; wars occurred earlier; social and political advances were postponed. By the time of advent of the Net the effects had smoothed out, as they always do, but the history of the species is bleaker than before. Intervention was abandoned and forbidden not in service to any fanciful ideal, *but out of despair— nothing* improves the lot of mankind in the past, or changes the overall course of history, however desperately we try!"

Sydney Jordan

Faces Showing the Stamp of Time

The letter is addressed to me, it is in my handwriting, and I cannot remember writing it or deciding to send it to myself. Everything about it is wrong.

A stamp dealer, of course, gets self-addressed letters all the time. My colleagues around the world have stocks of my labels, as I do of theirs, and on the day of issue of any new stamp they routinely buy a bundle of first-day covers and address a batch of them to me. When I started out as a boy, of course, the envelopes and later the labels were handwritten; later typewritten; but once I began to deal in sizable quantities, I moved swiftly on to printed labels and to rubber stamps. In thirty years, many rubber stamps bearing my name and address have been worn down into illegibility, before I went on to word-processors which could produce labels to order. And since I always have several made up, in reserve, there's always one to hand when I have to post a stamped-addressed-envelope for some ordinary purpose like requesting a receipt or proof of delivery.

In any case, this envelope is empty. Unsealed, with the flap turned in, as I normally do with s.a.e.'s in case I do want to enclose something in the future. It has all the signs of being one of my own, routine acquisitions, except for the handwriting. That is unusual.

Even stranger is the stamp. It bears a portrait of Prince Charles, and that in itself is striking: as any expert can tell you, a thematic collection on the royal children will scarcely fill a page of an album. Apart from the British commemoratives of the Investiture and his wedding, the rest will be from small countries capitalising on state visits. There are no British stamps showing simply the man himself. And yet at first glance this is a British stamp, because there is no other country's name on it. Under the conventions of the International Postal Union, the fact that Britain invented the postage stamp confers on us, and on no other nation, the curiously inverted privilege of *not* putting our name on our stamps. Instead, the rules state, every British stamp must bear the recognisable face of the reigning monarch. It has pushed the Queen's head into some strange places, in some ill-thought-out designs. Yet on this stamp, there is no Queen's head at all.

Furthermore, the denomination is two pounds, fifty pence. Now just about everyone knows that large denomination British stamps have castles on them. For all the effects of inflation, we are still far from the point where £2.50 would be the standard price for even a first-class letter. Even now, as I write in 1993, it would be more than a tenfold increase. I could explain it, offhand, in only one way: if I was present at an event of such consequence that I bought copies of every denomination of stamp and mailed them to myself in anticipation of profit—so many that I ran out of the labels I always carry. And one of those envelopes, by some bizarre circumstance, slid back in time to let me know what had happened.

But what was it? I can think of only one thing that would make it worth buying ordinary, day-by-day stamps in such quantities. In a time when the present Prince of Wales was King, I would have to be present at some event involving him so intimately that any stamp featuring him, and franked for that place and time, would be of commercial value.

And now comes the nightmare. The only event I can think of which might do it is a political assassination. The date makes sense: July 1st, 2009, the 40th anniversary of his Investiture as Prince of Wales. In that time, though I wish long life to Her Majesty like any loyal subject, it is entirely conceivable that she will have surrendered the throne to her firstborn son: an event he might well choose to commemorate after the Coronation, with an extra ceremony at Caernarvon, where his mother invested him forty years before. That is the place-name on the postmark, as clearly legible as the date. I can even set some boundaries on the time, because the collection was at 16.15 hours, and whatever happened must have happened at least an hour before—probably longer.

It would be a terrible blow to the nation. It amazes me, even now in my sixties, how few people remember the shock that ran through the land on the death of George VI; how amazed they are when I mention 'the King's Christmas broadcast' or 'drinking the King's health', as if the present Queen has always reigned and always will. Despite the warning of his long illness, people were shocked; telephone switchboards were jammed with queries; Britain went into mourning. A sudden death, especially by violence, would be much worse.

And I know, if not it all, at least enough probably to prevent it. If I do, of course, I will deny myself financial gain; but that is not everything. If that had been my only concern in life, I might have devoted it to larger concerns than dealing in postage stamps. I can truthfully say that I feel no temptation to keep silent for that reason. But what am I to do? If I step forward now, the stamp will be dismissed as a clumsy forgery, the rest the work of a madman. If I wait until the stamps are issued, the accusation will be only that I forged the postmark, easier still.

I am lodging this account now with a Notary Public, along with the envelope, in hopes that it will help to prove my story. My nightmare is that otherwise I will be standing in the crowd, an old man armed with a full set of the envelopes from which I will profit (because I must have them, and post them, for one to come back to me now) and I shall try to attract the attention first of the police, then of the Special Branch, with no evidence except for an envelope whose postmark will then be only an hour or so in the future.

They will thrust me back into the crowd; or, more probably,

eject me from the site altogether. It will let me reach a posting box ahead of whatever chaos ensues. The envelope will be launched on its way back to me through time, handwritten as it sits before me now, my address blurred only in the bottom right-hand corner, on the last digits of the postcode. Water has fallen on the envelope there: raindrops, perhaps, as the postman came up the steps to my door. There was rain this morning. Or then again, with no idea as I write of what will happen or how bad it will be—how many others, perhaps, will be victims—perhaps, sixteen years from now, those blurring drops may be my tears.

Galileo at the High Frontier

Bringing Galileo forward to 1979 was an experiment, a trial run for the much bigger project which would take him to the Galilean moons of our own time, the 3020s. Before he saw the reality, we thought to test his reaction to the first detailed images of the planet and its moons which humanity acquired, without (as we thought) any risk of altering history before and after.

How wrong we proved to be! We thought we could stop Galileo carrying any memory of the experience back to his own time, but we reckoned without the strength of his will. Now we have remedied the consequences sufficiently for the altered timeline to converge with our own, we leave this record of what happened in 1979 at the 2079 exhibition, as a warning to our future selves. The second experiment, which would have brought Copernicus, Kepler, Galileo, Newton and Huygens together in *conversazione* at the High Frontier, to see and discuss the results of the great decade of planetary exploration, must remain untried—at least by us. Legend says Copernicus never saw Mercury, hidden throughout his life by mists over the River Vistula. Had he seen the images from Mariner 10, learned of its 2:1 locked rotation and thence the true shape of its orbit, would he have anticipated Kepler—or would he have recoiled from the demonstration that the heavens are not laid out in divinely perfect circles? If he, too, carried memory of the shock back to his own time, the consequences might be severe.

We brought Galileo from 1611, when his discoveries were

controversial, but not yet thought heretical. We said we would take him to a place and a time where he could see Jupiter's moons as they truly are—as he had sarcastically wished Libri might see them, on his way to Heaven. He had announced their existence briefly at the end of *The Starry Messenger*, after the mountains of the Moon and the star fields of the Milky Way; and he had yet to publish the keys to his anagrams announcing the phases of Venus, and the supposed triple nature of Saturn. If he had questions about those, we thought, his guides could answer.

He knew he was in Scotland, though Glasgow had only eight streets in his time and meant nothing to him. We explained how, through our machines, he could speak and hear, understand and be understood. As guides, we enlisted the creators of the exhibition, not telling them they would lose memory of the event. (In that, at least, we were successful.) They were a motley trio, not dressed like the patrons nor the artisans of an artistic event in Galileo's time. The black-haired, bearded Lunan and the clean-shaven but otherwise ragged Roberts appeared to be wearing tent-cloth from Genoa, Lunan's new and pressed, the other's faded and patched, but both died blue; Braithwaite's corduroy trousers also looked Genoese, but his padded jacket looked like the undercoat for some futuristic armour, except for its shiny yellow colour. He spoke first, with formal politeness.

"Domino Signor Galilei, it is an honour to welcome you to our exhibition. As a maker of telescopes myself, I have long been in awe of what you have accomplished."

"I have no time for imitators," snapped Galileo. "I am the sole creator of the optic tube and the sole master of its use. Tell me about this exhibition that surrounds us. Does it commemorate some great man's achievement?"

"You could say that," Lunan replied, "though like your most distinguished successor, he stood upon the shoulders of giants..." and as he paused, Roberts added, "It's ten years since a man first walked upon the Moon—the exhibition portrays what has happened since."

"Walked upon the Moon?" Galileo was taken aback. "That fool Kepler, with his harmonies and invisible perfect solids—what was it he wrote to me... ?"

"*Let us create vessels and sails adjusted to the heavenly ether, and there will be plenty of people unafraid of the empty wastes,*" Lunan quoted. "*In the meantime, we shall prepare, for the bold sky-travellers, maps of the celestial bodies—I shall do it for the Moon, you, Galileo, for Jupiter.* I've used it in my next book."

"I wish him well in that attempt," said Galileo, "for I have yet to send him a 'telescope', as you call it, and I do not intend to do so. Do you have proof of this 'Moon-walking'?"

"Come and see this." Roberts led them across the great, white-painted hall to a display of images on a pillar, next to a glass case. Within it lay strange devices, the only recognisable features being the lenses. "These are Hasselblad cameras, and these are the images Neil Armstrong took with them on the Moon. They're all pictures of his companion, except for this one where Armstrong is reflected in his visor."

With no idea what was meant—camera? hidden things?—Galileo looked from the white suits of armour to Braithwaite's yellow padding, wondering if he, too, had walked on that rocky surface. But Roberts was in full flow, pointing out the highlights of the exhibition he had created. "That's a Lunar Orbiter image of the Moon—and over here, the Viking photographs of Mars..."

"And 'Moons of Mars'!" Galileo exclaimed. "Kepler mis-translated my Saturn anagram as *Hail, burning twins, offspring of Mars...*"

"He was right," Lunan replied, "and that wasn't the only time! You'd better come to see Jupiter."

They crossed back over the hall to the entrance, turning to show Galileo the full sweep of the central display board. "This picture is only seven months old," said Lunan. "It was taken by a spacecraft called Voyager 1. South is at the top, as you would see in your telescope. The moons in front are..."

"Damnation to the moons!" shouted Galileo, pointing in fury at the Great Red Spot, dominating the picture with Io silhouetted against it. "What in the name of God is that?"

"It's a circular storm on Jupiter, three times the size of Earth. It's been there for at least three hundred years—"

"Kepler knew of it! He decoded my Venus anagram to read, *There is a red spot in Jupiter which rotates mathematically!*"

"Coincidence," said Roberts. "It couldn't be anything else—"

"Have I been brought here only to see how many times Kepler was right? Right about the Moon, right about Mars, right about Jupiter! I build the instruments, I damage my back and my eyesight conducting detailed research, and he comes along with his mystical numbers and his witch of a mother, to make greater discoveries by decoding my anagrams wrongly?" He swung an arm at the blowup of Io and the panels of the Jovian satellites beyond. "My moons! My discoveries, whose reality you brought me here to see. Has he annexed them too? Are they Kepler's Stars, or do they still honour the Medici as I specified?"

"Political dedications seldom last," said Lunan. "Herschel tried to name Uranus after George the Third—"

"Not the point," Braithwaite interrupted. "They have individual names, after the classical companions of Jupiter, but collectively, almost from the outset, they've been called the Galilean moons. History has named them after you!"

"After me!" Galileo's mood changed, but not to anything more cordial. The word *braggadocio* might have been coined for him. "Ha! Do you hear that?" he shouted to the people in the hallway, "the Galilean moons!" Who knows what they made of it, since they were outside the translation field. "I've been too modest, too circumspect! I must confront my critics directly, especially those fools who surround the Pope. A Dialogue, that's the answer! I'll highlight their folly, I'll put their arguments into the mouths of a simpleton. Simplicius! That's the name for them! Simplicius!" The experiment was going badly awry, and we pulled him from the scene, still mouthing boastful threats as he vanished.

"That didn't go very well," said Lunan. "I wanted him to meet Edwin Morgan—to hear *Galileo would have been proud of Ganymede*, at least."

"I wanted to show him the six-inch reflector in the annexe," said Braithwaite. "To discuss optics with *Galileo…*"

"I wanted to get a picture of him, before he popped off," said Roberts.

"Your disappointment will pass." Coming from the shadows, we took their memories, left them staring at nothing, and were gone.

The rest is history. Not the history they knew, where Galileo died the most honoured man in Europe, and not the history that replaced it, where he burned at the stake for his presumption, but the one *you* know, where we have repaired the damage as best we could. When you come near to our time, when you discover the power to change the past, be warned and do not meddle further.

Inspired by, and perhaps a prequel to, *Galileo's Dream* by Kim Stanley Robinson (HarperVoyager, 2009). For the rest of the background see *The Sleepwalkers* by Arthur Koestler (Hutchinson, 1959).

Notes

In 1978-79 I was the Manager of the Glasgow Parks Astronomy Project, with the late John Braithwaite (afterwards the last maker of telescopes in Scotland) as Technical Supervisor, and Gavin Roberts (now Principal Teacher of Art at Airdrie Academy) as Art and Photographic Spervisor. Our initial brief in 1978 was to build an astronomical monument in one of the city's parks, as a Jobs Creation project, and that became the first astronomically aligned stone circle for over 3000 years. Its story up to mid-2012 is told in my book "The Stones and the Stars" (Springer, 2012), and the subsequent campaign to save it from redevelopment is on my website, www.duncanlunan.com.

In the second half of 1978 we found ourselves under increasing demand to provide talks and exhibitions for schools and public libraries, and in 1979 the project's remit was broadened to 'Astronomy and Space Education', with a total staff of ten including illustrator Dave McClymont and draughtsman Richard Robertson, with the late Bill Braithwaite (John's father) as model-maker. One of the major commitments was to create the exhibition 'The High Frontier, a Decade of Space Research', using the photo-archives of ASTRA, the Association in Scotland to Research into Astronautics, and the facilities of the Third Eye Centre on Sauchiehall Street, Glasgow (now the Centre for Contemporary Arts), whose Director, Chris Carrel, had previously run the very successful 'Beyond This Horizon' space and science fiction festival at the Ceolfrith Arts Centre in Sunderland.

The High Frontier (taking its title from the book by the late Prof. Gerard K. O'Neill) was the largest event of its kind in the UK to date, and of three such events planned in the UK by various groups for the tenth anniversary of the Moon landing, it was the only one to reach fulfilment. It was supported by NASA, the European Space Agency, British Aerospace, Rockwell International Inc., British Telecom, Hasselblad, the Smithsonian Air and Space Museum and many other contributors. Its centrepieces were two large blowups of the new Voyager images of Jupiter and Io, sponsored by the *Glasgow Herald*. In the summer of 1979 I undertook a whirlwind tour of US space centres and contractors to gather exhibits, financed by the Scottish Arts Council, and I've described parts of that in *Man and the Planets* (Ashgrove Press, 1983) and in *Waverider, A Spacecraft in Waiting* in preparation).

As well as numerous talks the programme included seminars on astronomy, science fiction writing, applications satellites, Space & Scotland (an ongoing enquiry today), and nuclear waste disposal in space, reconsidered in my book *Incoming Asteroid!* (Springer, 2013). Two books were produced at the time, a collection of essays edited by Bob Low of the *Daily Record*, and *Star Gate, the Science Fiction Poetry of Edwin Morgan*. There was a programme of science fiction films at the Glasgow Film Theatre with accompanying documentaries, talks and an overspill exhibition.

From Glasgow the exhibition went on tour around the UK, and was estimated to have been seen by around 86,000 people. Elements of it continued to be shown at science fiction conventions and other exhibitions through to the 1990s, as the chipboard-mounted panels were systematically replaced with more portable ones by Chris O'Kane and Richard McKelvie of ASTRA, financed by the Glasgow SF conventions. Finally the Jupiter blowups were purchased by the Glasgow Museum of Transport and the whole exhibition was replaced in 1995 by Gordon Ross at Glasgow School of Art. Panels of Hannes Giger's artwork for *Alien* were shown again at the 1987 World Science Fiction Convention in Brighton, and original artwork by Sydney Jordan for the *Jeff Hawke* and *Lance McLane* comic strips was incorporated into the 'Urban Spacemen' exhibition of space art by Scots, which appeared at the 90s Gallery during Glasgow's year as European City of Culture in 1990, later at other venues including the Orkney and Caithness Science Festivals, the Lantern Gallery in Stornoway and finally at the 1996 Edinburgh International Science Festival.

For the High Frontier Bill Braithwaite created a model of the Waverider re-entry vehicle, designed by the late Prof. Terence Nonweiler, and its showing at the High Frontier in Largs in 1981 led to the formation of ASTRA's Waverider Aerodynamic Study Programme, whose story I hope to tell in *Waverider, a Spacecraft in Waiting*.

To sum up, the High Frontier was a major effort, whose echoes are still ringing today. I was therefore very pleased when I was asked to write a time-travel story, set at the exhibition, for *To Arrive at Where We Started*, edited by Laura Smith in 2012 for a retrospective CCA exhibition on its Third Eye Centre years. The year before I had reviewed *Galileo's Dream*, by Kim Stanley Robinson, for *Concatenation*, and that gave me part of my inspiration.

The other element was that over the years, John Braithwaite and I had talked about putting on a drama production at the High Frontier or its successors, as a *conversazione* in which actors playing Copernicus, Tycho Brahe, Kepler, Galileo and Newton would discuss the exhibits with one another and with a live audience at the exhibition. Much of their dialogue would be drawn from *The Sleepwalkers* by Arthur Koestler. The idea was discussed with playwrights, producers and actors at various times, but never quite came off.

Putting it together with the ideas of *Galileo's Dream* and the CCA commission, however, the story virtually wrote itself, and was a great opportunity to recall our younger selves as the Astronomy Project's three main participants. My only regret is that John Braithwaite, who died suddenly and sadly in February 2012, did not live to see it.

Thomas Brash

About the Author

Duncan Lunan was born in Edinburgh in 1945 and grew up in Troon, Ayrshire, attending Marr College and Glasgow University. In 1968 he graduated as M.A. with Honours in English and Philosophy, with Physics, Astronomy and French as supporting subjects, and has a postgraduate Diploma in Education. In 1970 he became a full-time author, initially writing science fiction, then broadened his range to nonfiction with emphasis on astronomy, spaceflight and science fiction; he also undertakes a wide range of other writing and speaking as a researcher, tutor, critic, editor, lecturer and broadcaster. His book *Children from the Sky: a speculative investigation of a mediaeval mystery, the Green Children of Woolpit* was published by Mutus Liber in May 2012 (see Duncan's website, www. duncanlunan.com, and www.childrenfromthesky.co.uk.) and was followed by two books for Springer, *The Stones and the Stars: a new stone circle for Scotland*, and *Incoming Asteroid! What could we do about it?*, published in November 2012 and 2013.

His earlier publications include three nonfiction books, contributions to 32 other books, nearly 1250 articles and 36 short stories, including ten for the comic strip *Lance McLane*, created by Sydney Jordan for the *Daily Record*. He was science fiction critic of the *Glasgow Herald* 1971-85 and ran its annual science fiction and fantasy short story competition 1986-92, followed each year by a creative writing course at Glasgow University's Department of Adult & Continuing Education. That led in turn to the formation of the Glasgow Science Fiction Writers' Circle, still flourishing 30 years later. In 1989 he edited *Starfield: science fiction by Scottish writers*, the first ever anthology of SF and fantasy by Scots, and for *Jeff Hawke's Cosmos*, which is reprinting the world's longest-running SF comic strip, he contributes notes on the stories as they appear. He reviews fiction for *Interzone* and *Shoreline of Infinity*, and non-fiction for *Concatenation*. His regular astronomy column *The Sky Above You* appears in several newspapers and magazines.

As Manager of the Glasgow Parks Dept. Astronomy Project, 1978-79, Duncan designed and built the first astronomically aligned stone circle in Britain for over 3000 years, which has been removed to make way for development, but will be re-created nearby. For updates see Duncan's website, and the Facebook page 'Friends of Sighthill Stone Circle'. From 1963 to 2010 he was a Council Member of ASTRA, the Association in Scotland to Research into Astronautics, a Curator of Airdrie Public Observatory 1980-81, 1987-97 and 2005-2008, and in 2006-2009 he ran an educational outreach project from the Observatory to schools, funded by the National Lottery. His other interests include ancient and mediaeval history, jazz, folk music and hillwalking.

After 30 years living in Glasgow, in 2012 Duncan returned to his home town of Troon, where he now lives with his wife Linda. He is the chairman of "Troon Writers" and of the "Astronomers of the Future Club" for beginners, also of the charity ACTA SCIO which oversees the AOTF and the campaign for the stone circle's reconstruction (www.actascio.org).

About the Illustrator

Sydney Jordan was born in Dundee and trained with Miles Aircraft before moving to Fleet Street, where he created 'Jeff Hawke', the world's longest-running science fiction strip cartoon, 1954-1988, for *The Daily Express*, later for *Scottish Daily News*, followed by 'Lance McLane' for *The Daily Record*, which became a reincarnation *of Jeff Hawke* elsewhere; both were syndicated in Europe and beyond, and three collections of Jeff Hawke stories have been published by Titan Books. The complete 'Jeff Hawke' has been published in book form in Italy, and there is now a Jeff Hawke Club reprinting the stories in magazine and book form in the UK, for which Duncan Lunan writes the accompanying 'Hawke's Notes'— visit www.jeffhawkeclub.co.uk to find out more.

Sydney's other strip credits include *Time and Ms Jones*, for the *Sunday Times*, the rebirth of *Dan Dare* for the short-lived *Sunday Planet*, and *Hal Starr*, now re-published in book form in Italy.

Sydney frequently illustrated articles in *The Daily Express* and his work has appeared in many newspapers and magazines including *New Worlds*, *Starburst* and *The Sunday Times*.

Subsequently he worked in advertising and the film industry and his credits include some of the story-boards for *Independence Day*.

He has illustrated articles and stories by Duncan Lunan in *World Magazine*, *The Journal of Practical Applications in Space*, *Asgard*, *Nuclear Free Scotland*, *Analog Science Fiction/Science Fact* and *Jeff Hawke's Cosmos*, created the cover painting for *Starfield: science fiction by Scottish writers*, edited by Duncan for Orkney Press, and illustrated Duncan's book *Children from the Sky*.

More of his artwork is included in Duncan's most recent book, *Incoming Asteroid! What Could We Do About It?*

Shoreline of Infinity Publications

We publish science fiction

To find out more, visit our website

www.shorelineofinfinity.com

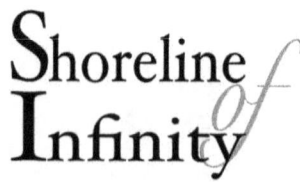

Shoreline of Infinity
Science fiction magazine
published in Scotland

www.shorelineofinfinity.com

www.ingramcontent.com/pod-product-compliance
Lightning Source LLC
Chambersburg PA
CBHW070302120726
47910CB00007B/2352